SUPER POTATO

#1 THE EPIC ORIGIN OF SUPER POTATO

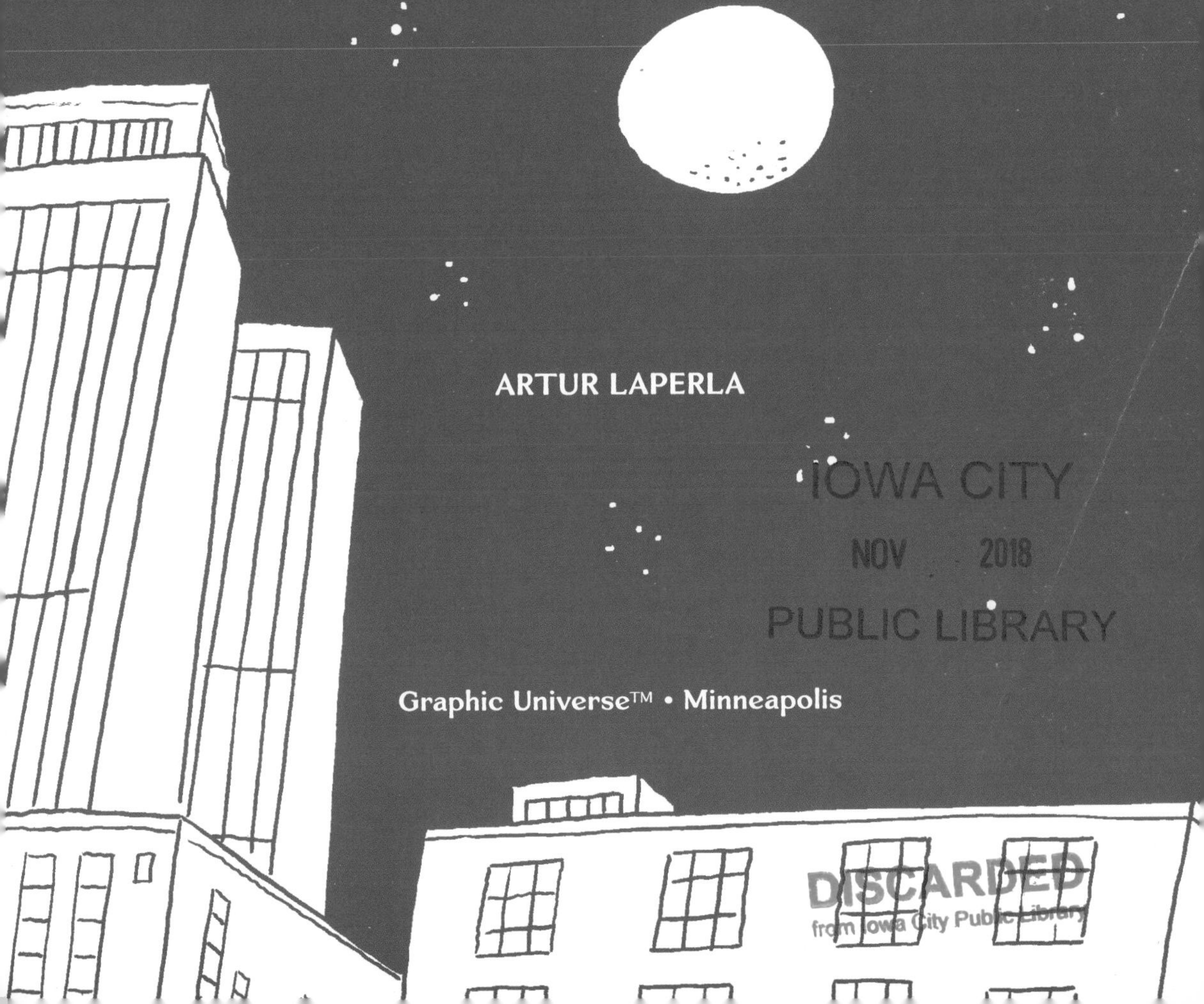

ARTUR LAPERLA

Graphic Universe™ • Minneapolis

Story and illustrations by Artur Laperla
Translation coordinated by Graphic Universe™

First American edition published in 2018 by Graphic Universe™

Graphic Universe™
A division of Lerner Publishing Group, Inc.
241 First Avenue North
Minneapolis, MN 55401 USA

For reading levels and more information, look up this title at www.lernerbooks.com.

Main body text set in CCWildWords 8.5/10. Typeface provided by Comicraft.

Library of Congress Cataloging-in-Publication Data

Names: Laperla (Artist) author, illustrator.
Title: The epic origin of Super Potato / Artur Laperla.
Description: First American edition. | Minneapolis : Graphic Universe, 2018. | Series: Super
    Potato ; #1 | Summary: After Doctor Malevolent turns him into a potato, Super Max must
    learn how to fight crime as a vegetable. | Identifiers: LCCN 2017043534 (print) | LCCN
    2017055277 (ebook) | ISBN 9781541523791 (eb pdf) | ISBN 9781512440218 (lb : alk. paper) |
    ISBN 9781541526457 (pb : alk. paper)
Subjects: LCSH: Graphic novels. | CYAC: Superheroes—Fiction. | Potatoes—Fiction. |
    Humorous stories. | Graphic novels.
Classification: LCC PZ7.7.L367 (ebook) | LCC PZ7.7.L367 Ep 2018 (print) | DDC 741.5/973—dc23

LC record available at https://lccn.loc.gov/2017043534

Manufactured in the United States of America
1-42290-26140-11/7/2017

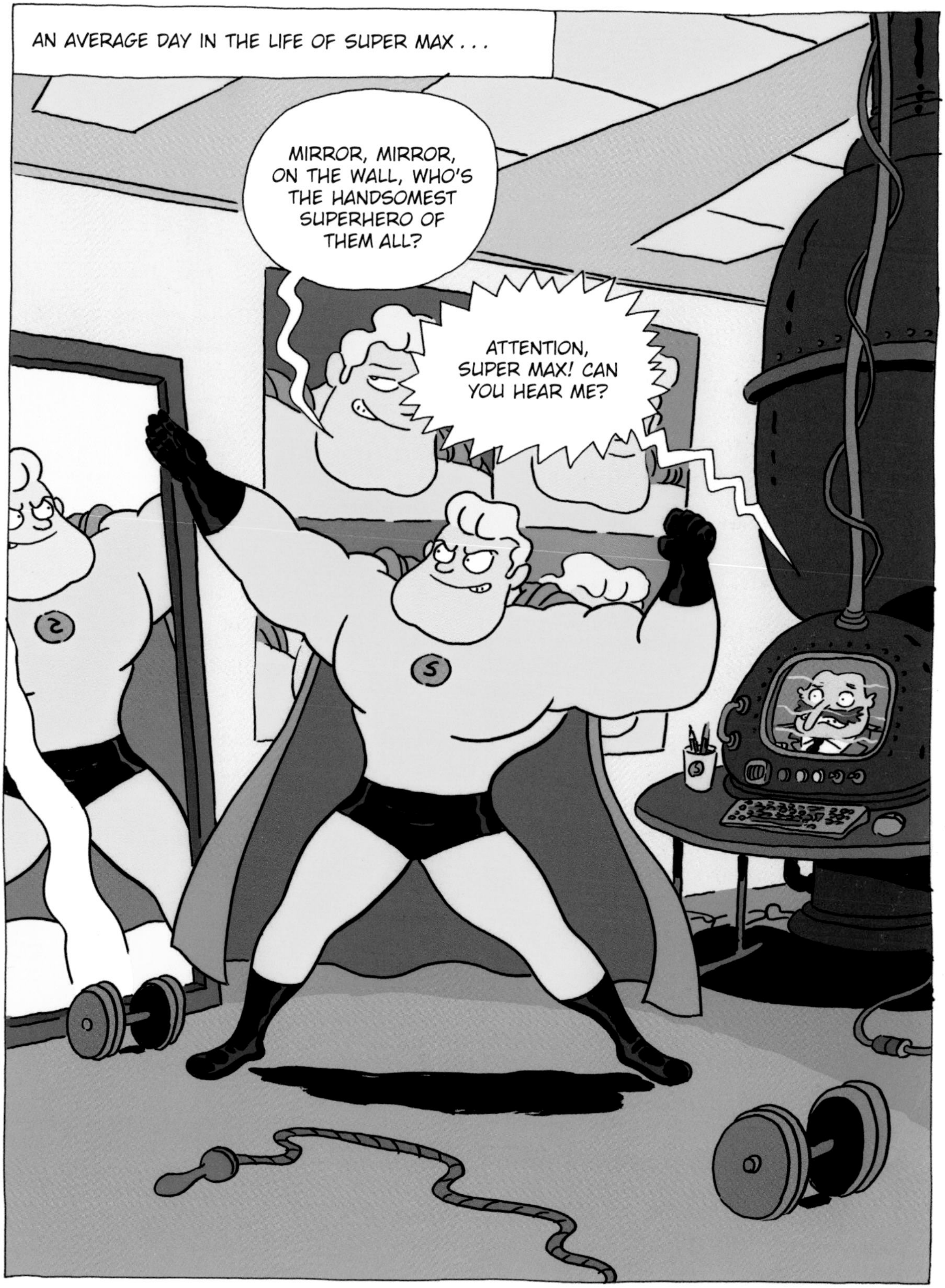
AN AVERAGE DAY IN THE LIFE OF SUPER MAX . . .
MIRROR, MIRROR, ON THE WALL, WHO'S THE HANDSOMEST SUPERHERO OF THEM ALL?
ATTENTION, SUPER MAX! CAN YOU HEAR ME?

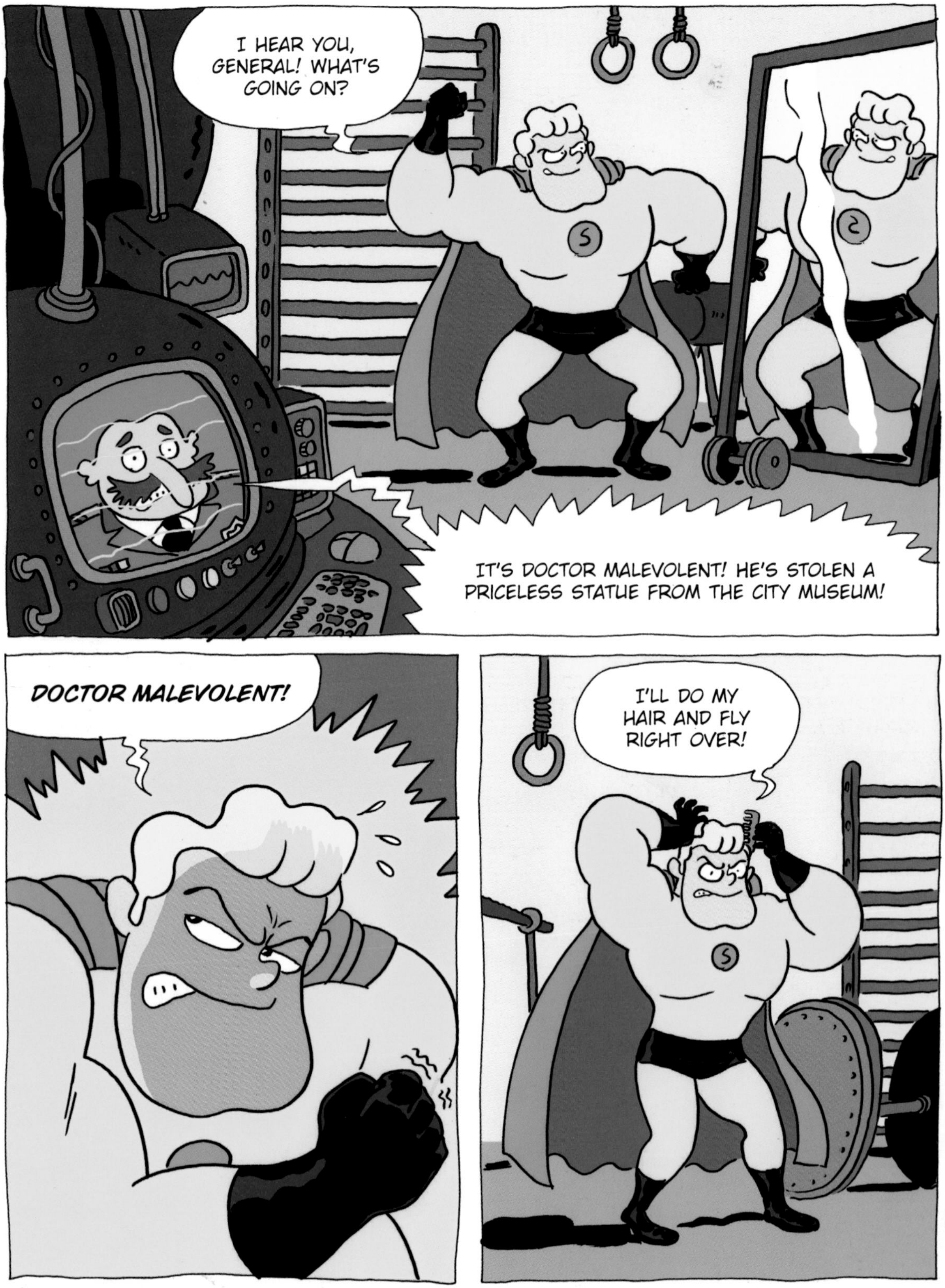
I HEAR YOU, GENERAL! WHAT'S GOING ON?
IT'S DOCTOR MALEVOLENT! HE'S STOLEN A PRICELESS STATUE FROM THE CITY MUSEUM!
DOCTOR MALEVOLENT!
I'LL DO MY HAIR AND FLY RIGHT OVER!

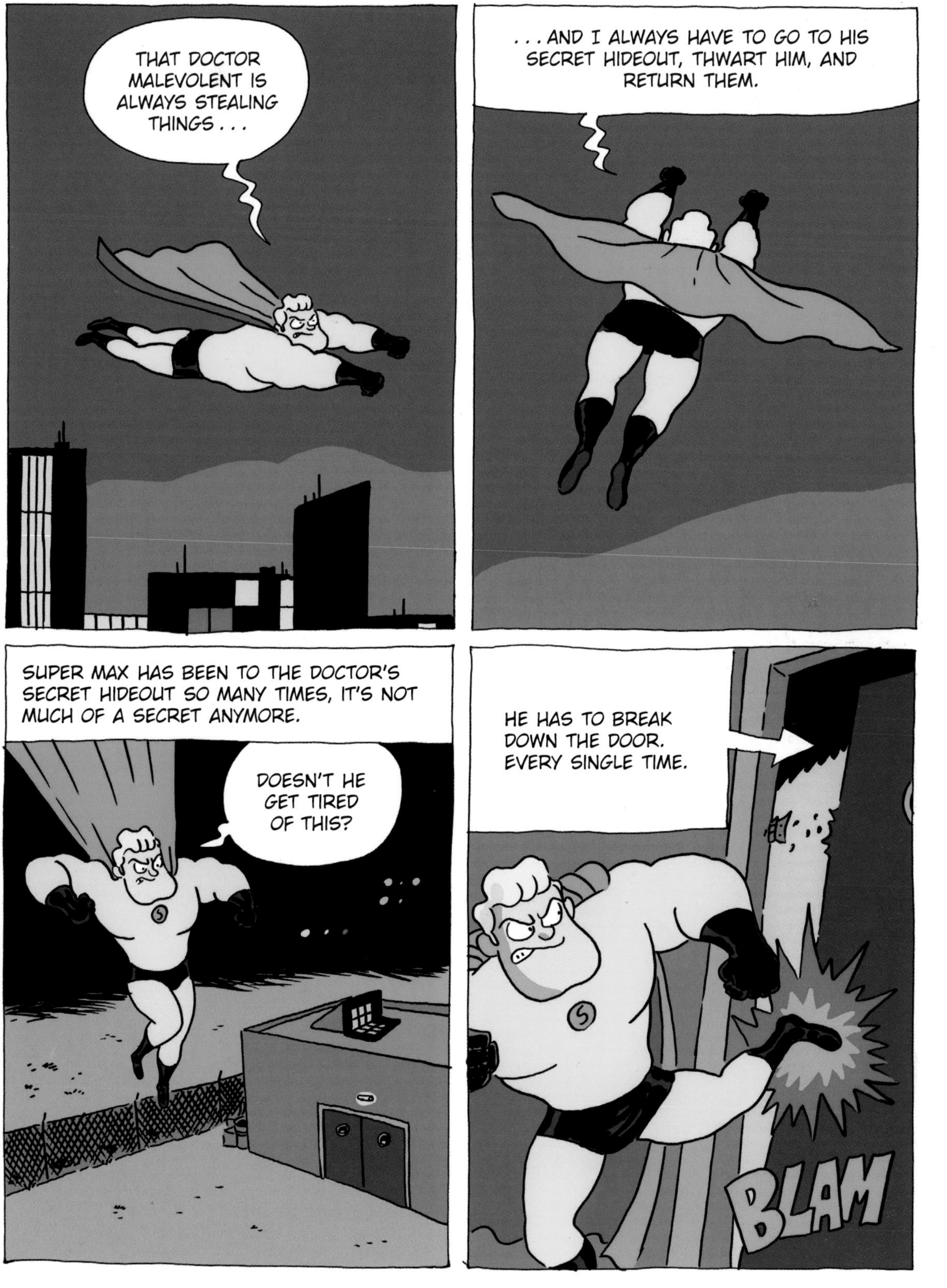
THAT DOCTOR MALEVOLENT IS ALWAYS STEALING THINGS . . .
. . . AND I ALWAYS HAVE TO GO TO HIS SECRET HIDEOUT, THWART HIM, AND RETURN THEM.
SUPER MAX HAS BEEN TO THE DOCTOR'S SECRET HIDEOUT SO MANY TIMES, IT'S NOT MUCH OF A SECRET ANYMORE.
DOESN'T HE GET TIRED OF THIS?
HE HAS TO BREAK DOWN THE DOOR. EVERY SINGLE TIME.
BLAM

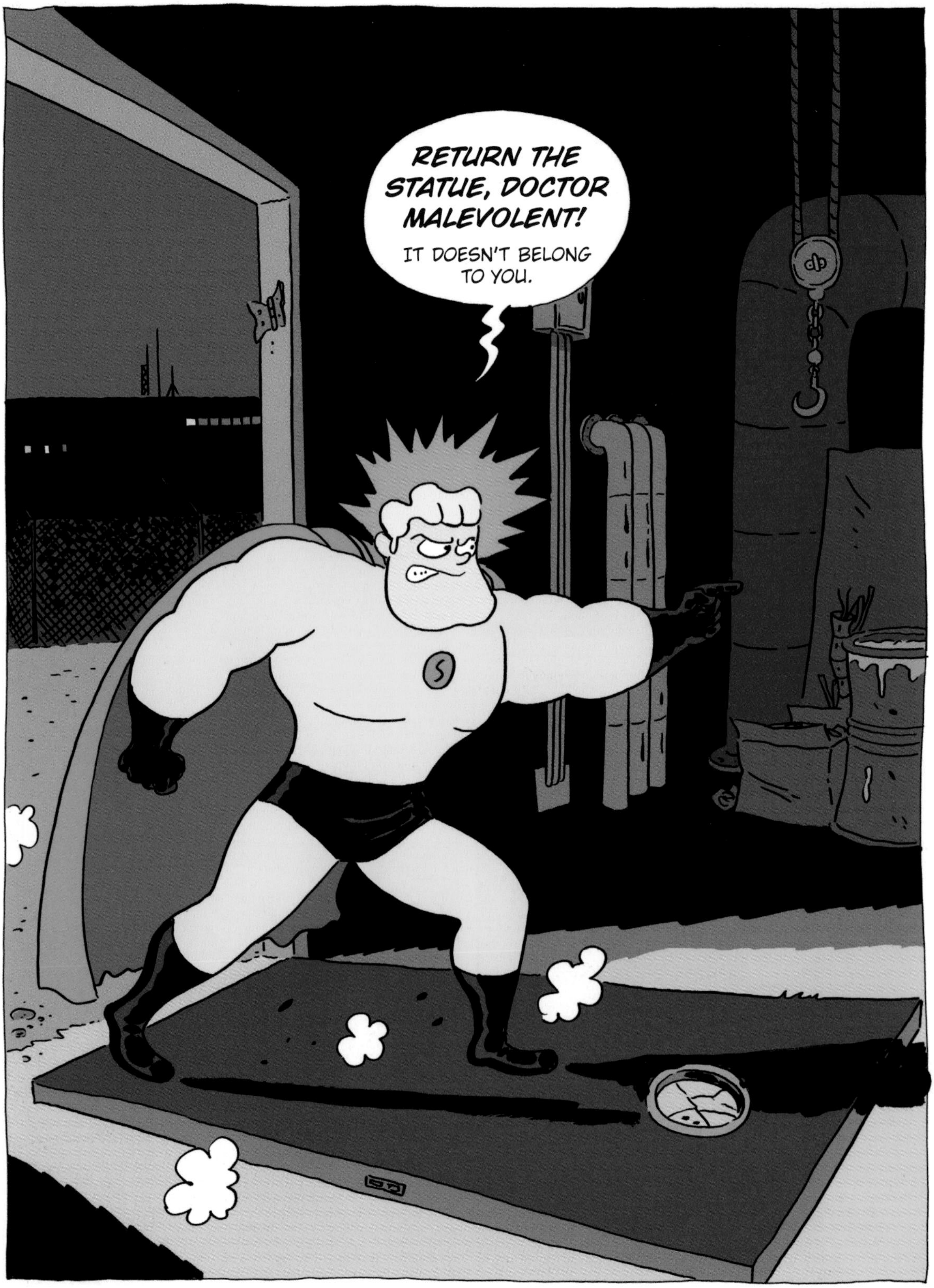
RETURN THE STATUE, DOCTOR MALEVOLENT!
IT DOESN'T BELONG TO YOU.

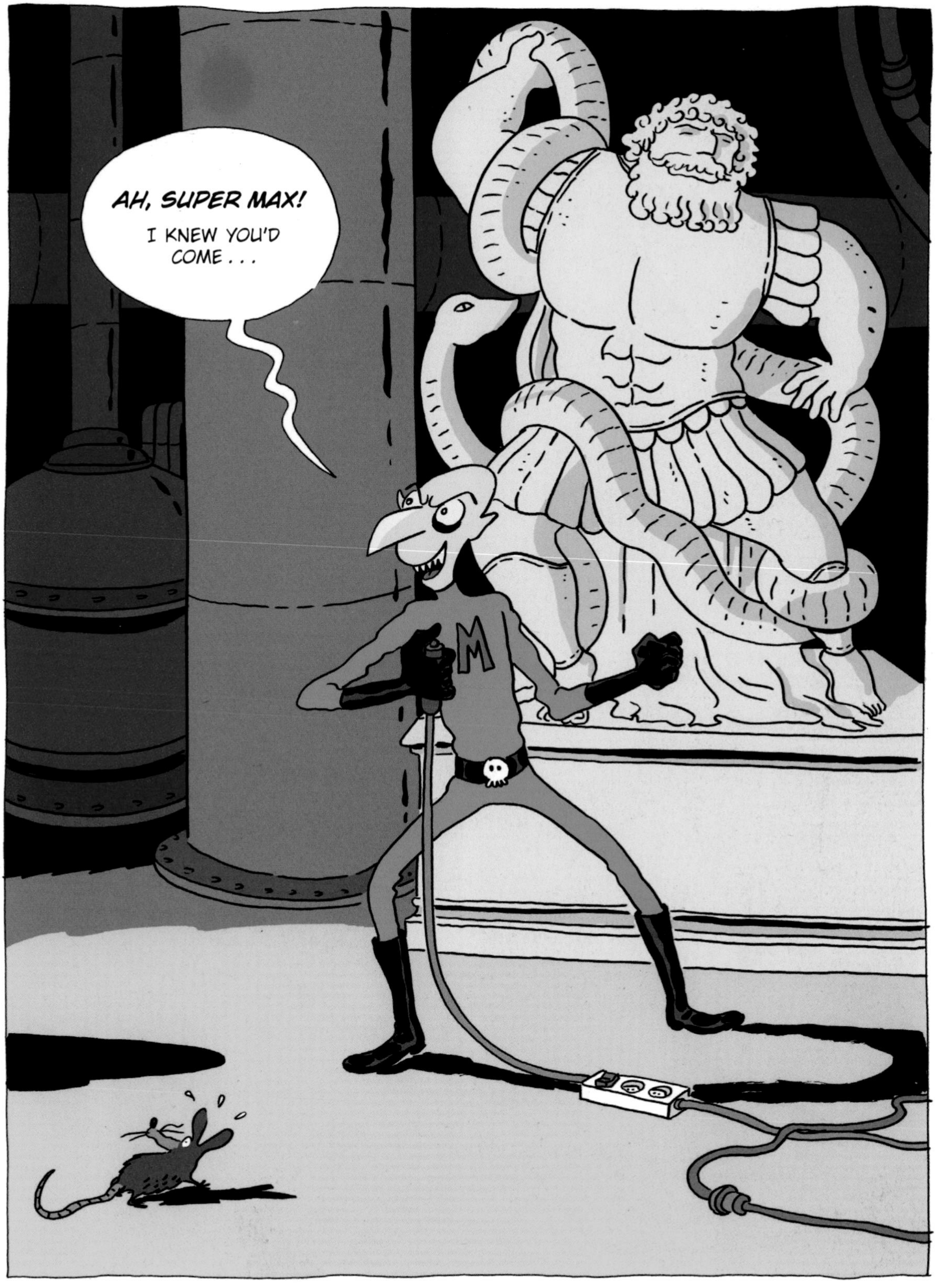
AH, SUPER MAX! I KNEW YOU'D COME . . .

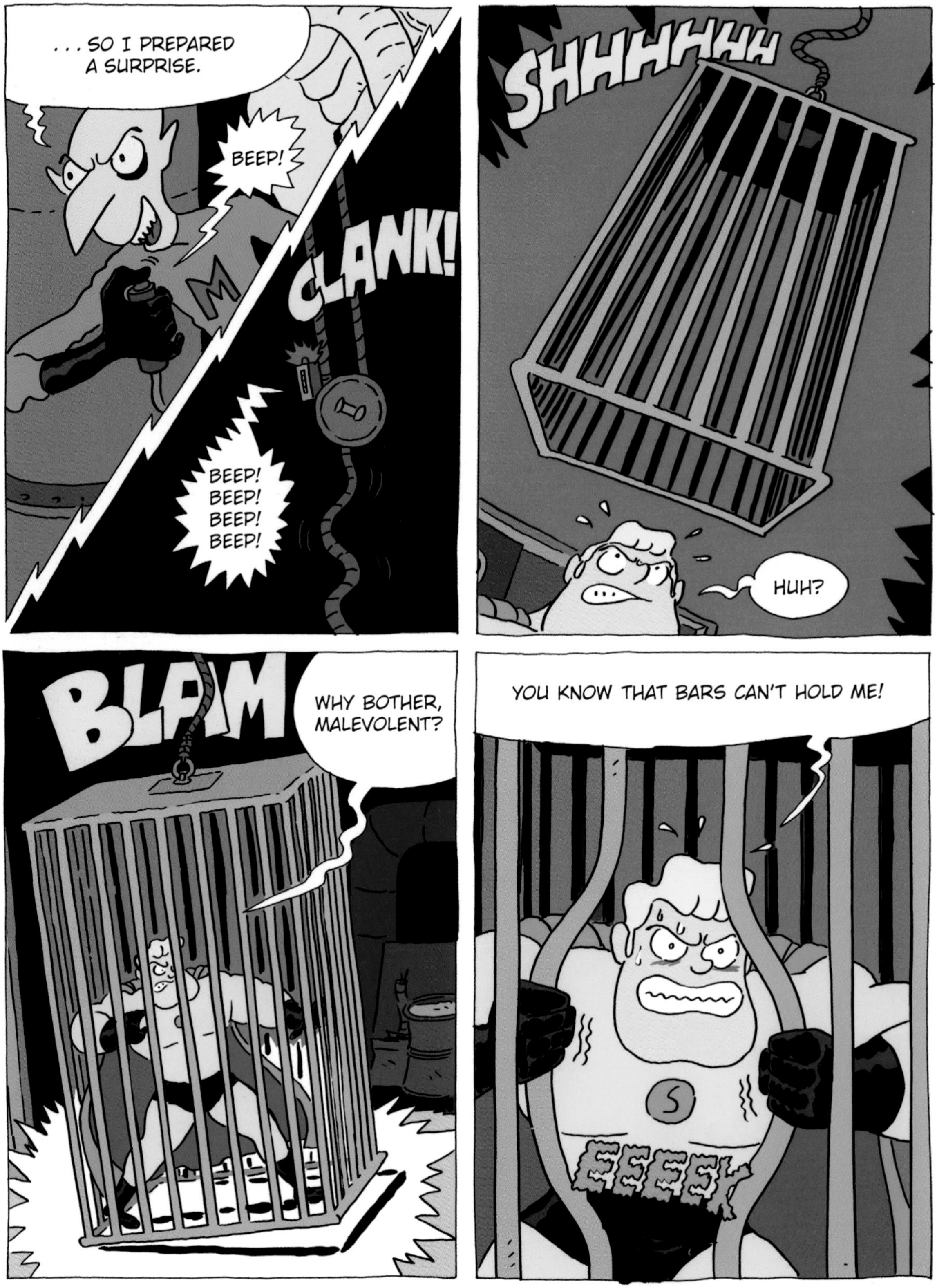
. . . SO I PREPARED A SURPRISE.
BEEP!
CLANK!
BEEP! BEEP! BEEP! BEEP!
SHHHHHH
HUH?
BLAM
WHY BOTHER, MALEVOLENT?
YOU KNOW THAT BARS CAN'T HOLD ME!
EEEEK

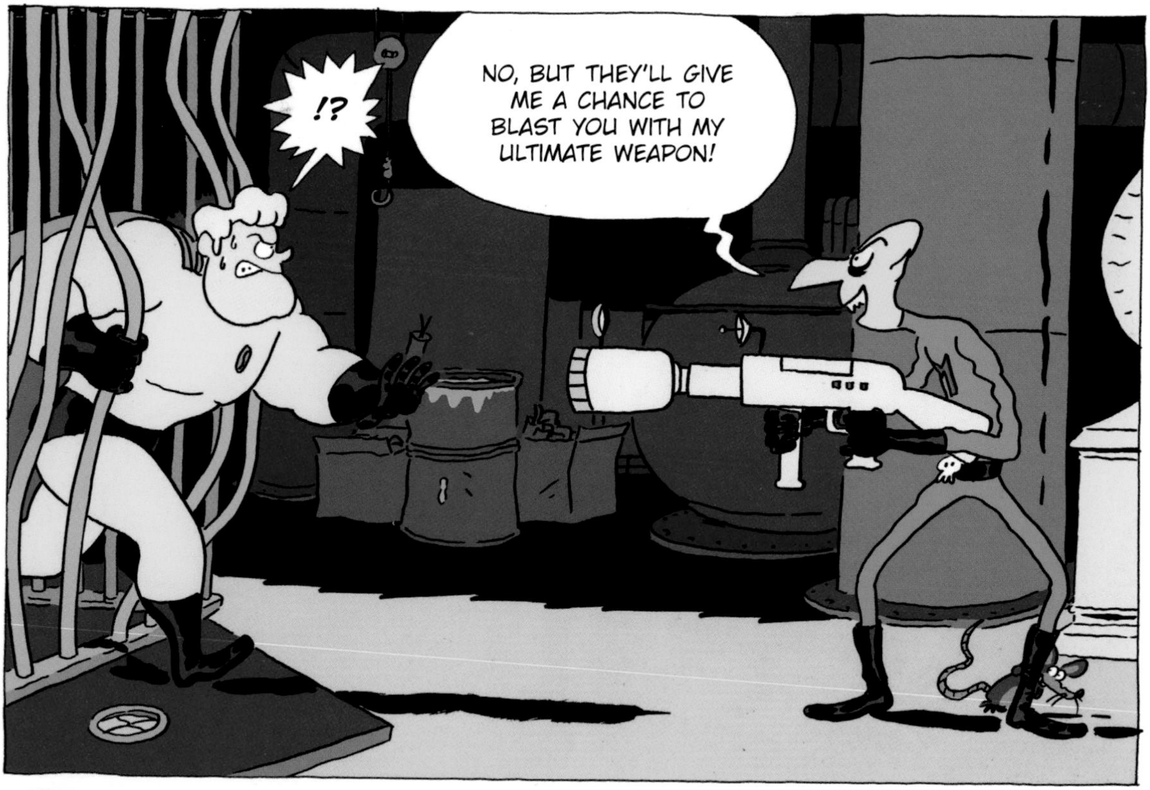
!?
NO, BUT THEY'LL GIVE ME A CHANCE TO BLAST YOU WITH MY ULTIMATE WEAPON!

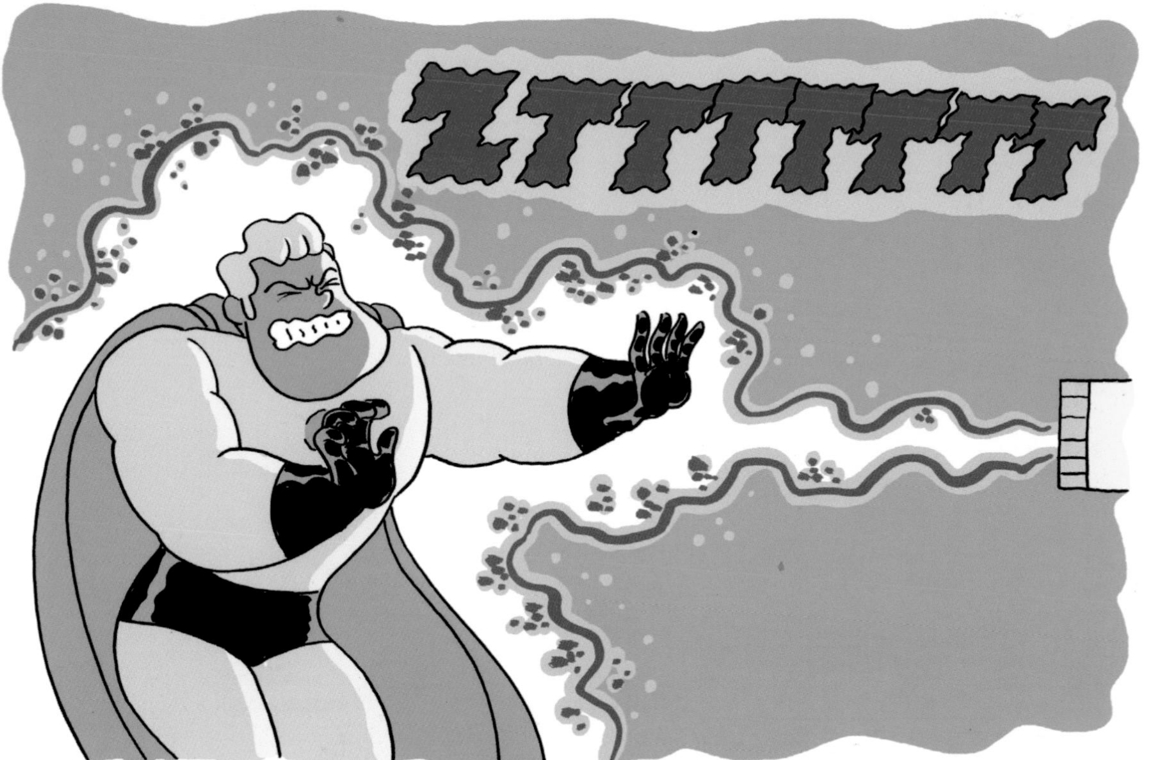
ZTTTTTTT

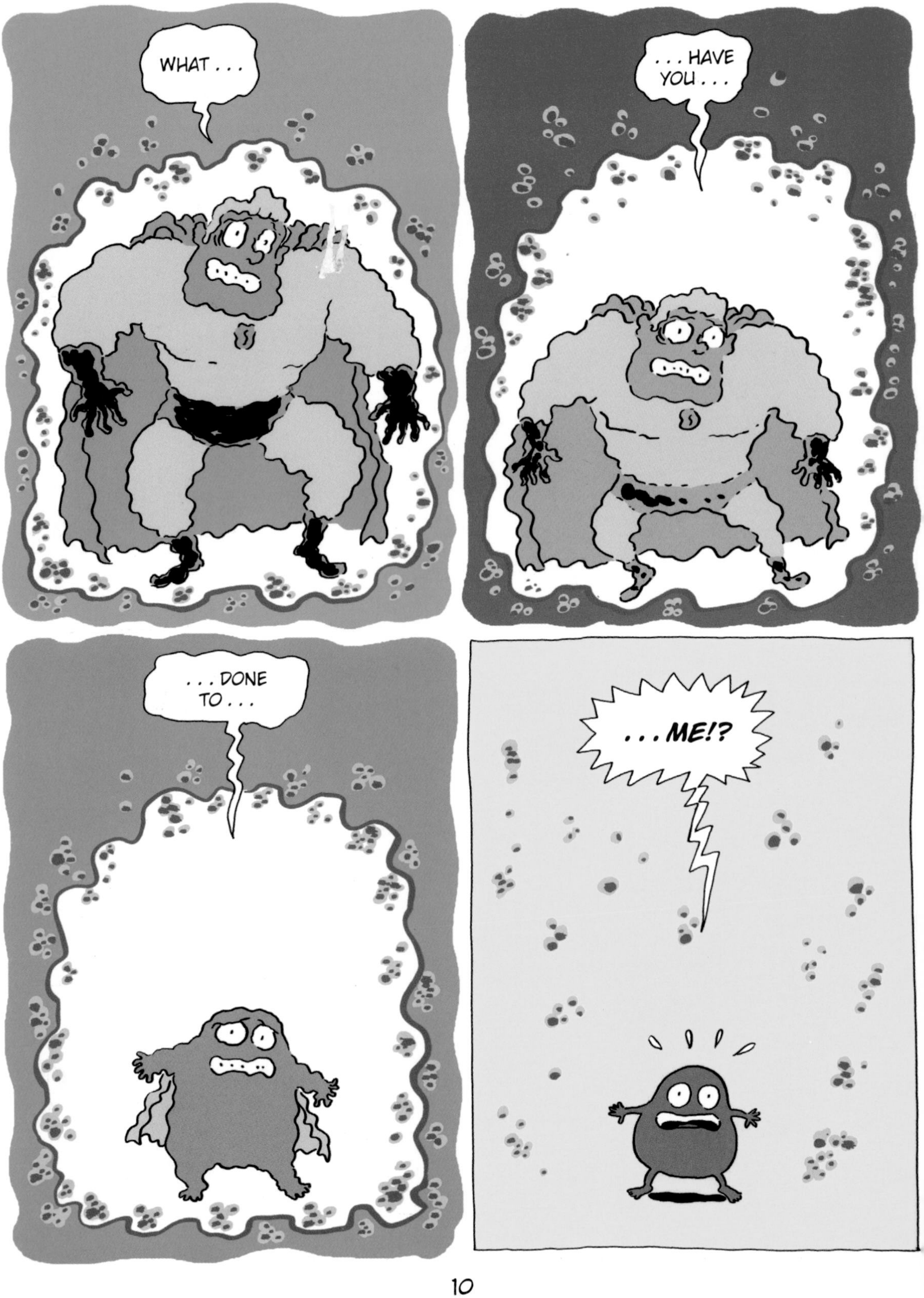
WHAT . . .
. . . HAVE YOU . . .
. . . DONE TO . . .
. . . ME!?

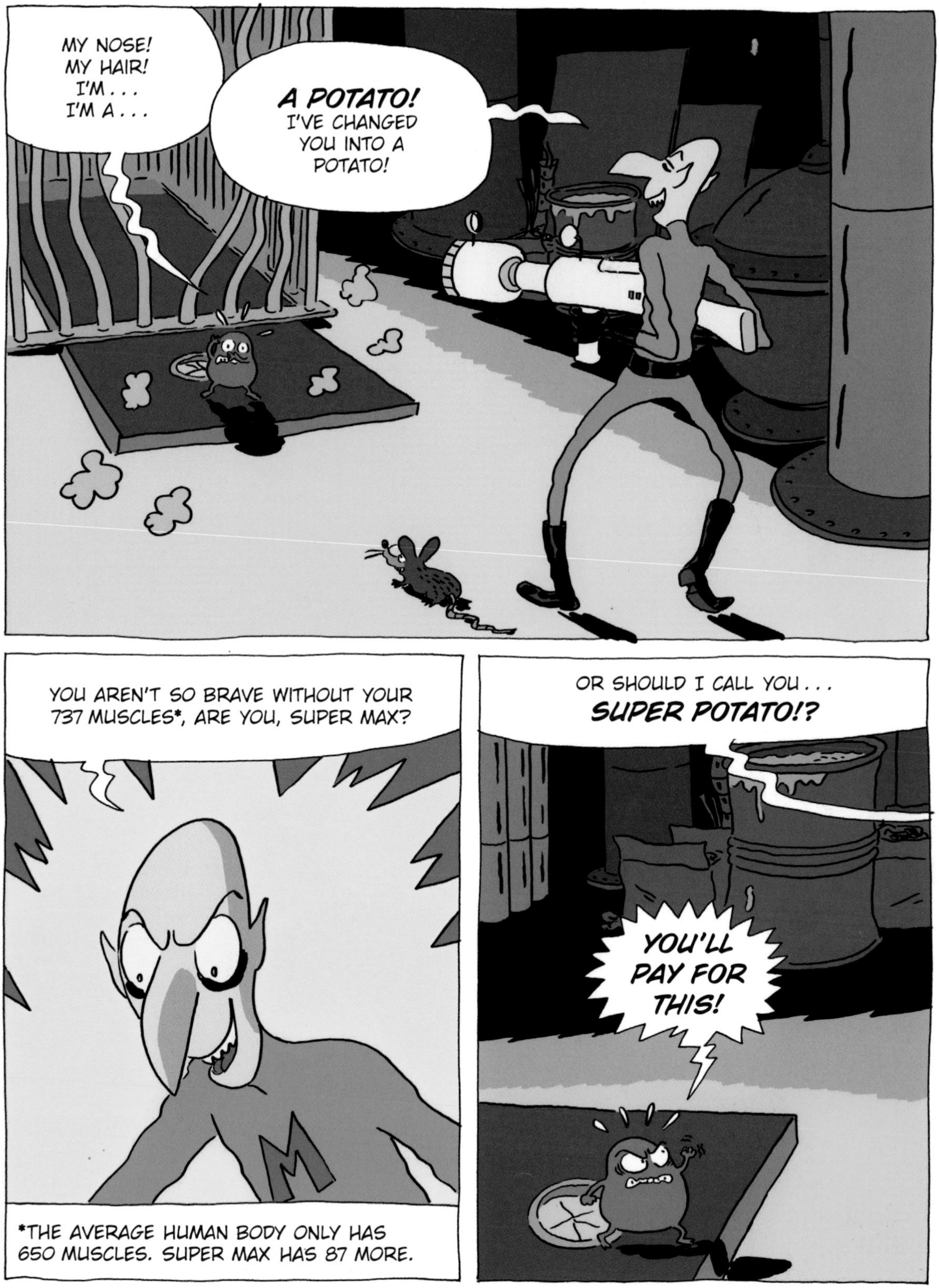
MY NOSE! MY HAIR! I'M . . . I'M A . . .
A POTATO! I'VE CHANGED YOU INTO A POTATO!
YOU AREN'T SO BRAVE WITHOUT YOUR 737 MUSCLES*, ARE YOU, SUPER MAX?
*THE AVERAGE HUMAN BODY ONLY HAS 650 MUSCLES. SUPER MAX HAS 87 MORE.
OR SHOULD I CALL YOU . . . SUPER POTATO!?
YOU'LL PAY FOR THIS!

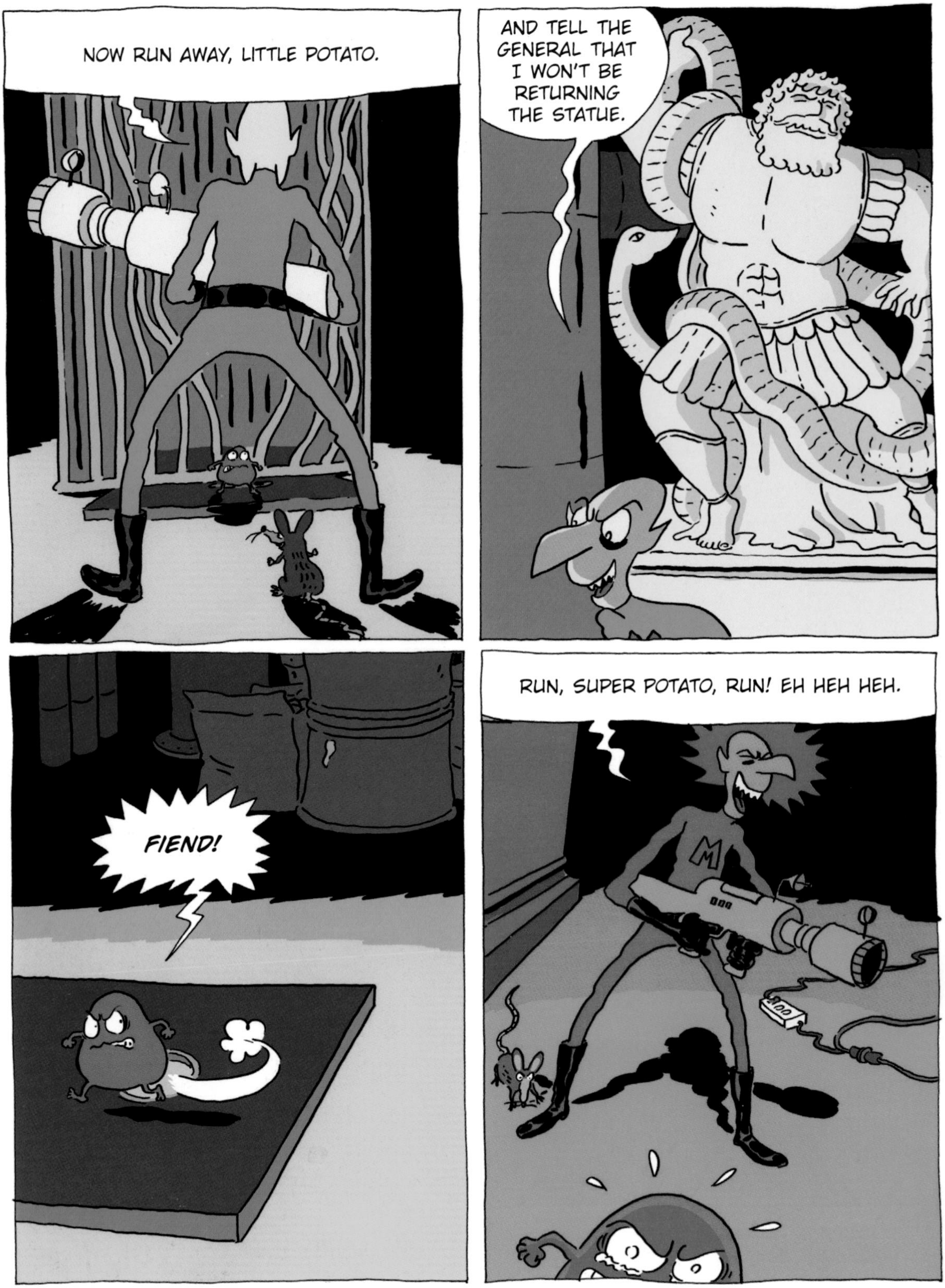
NOW RUN AWAY, LITTLE POTATO.
AND TELL THE GENERAL THAT I WON'T BE RETURNING THE STATUE.
FIEND!
RUN, SUPER POTATO, RUN! EH HEH HEH.

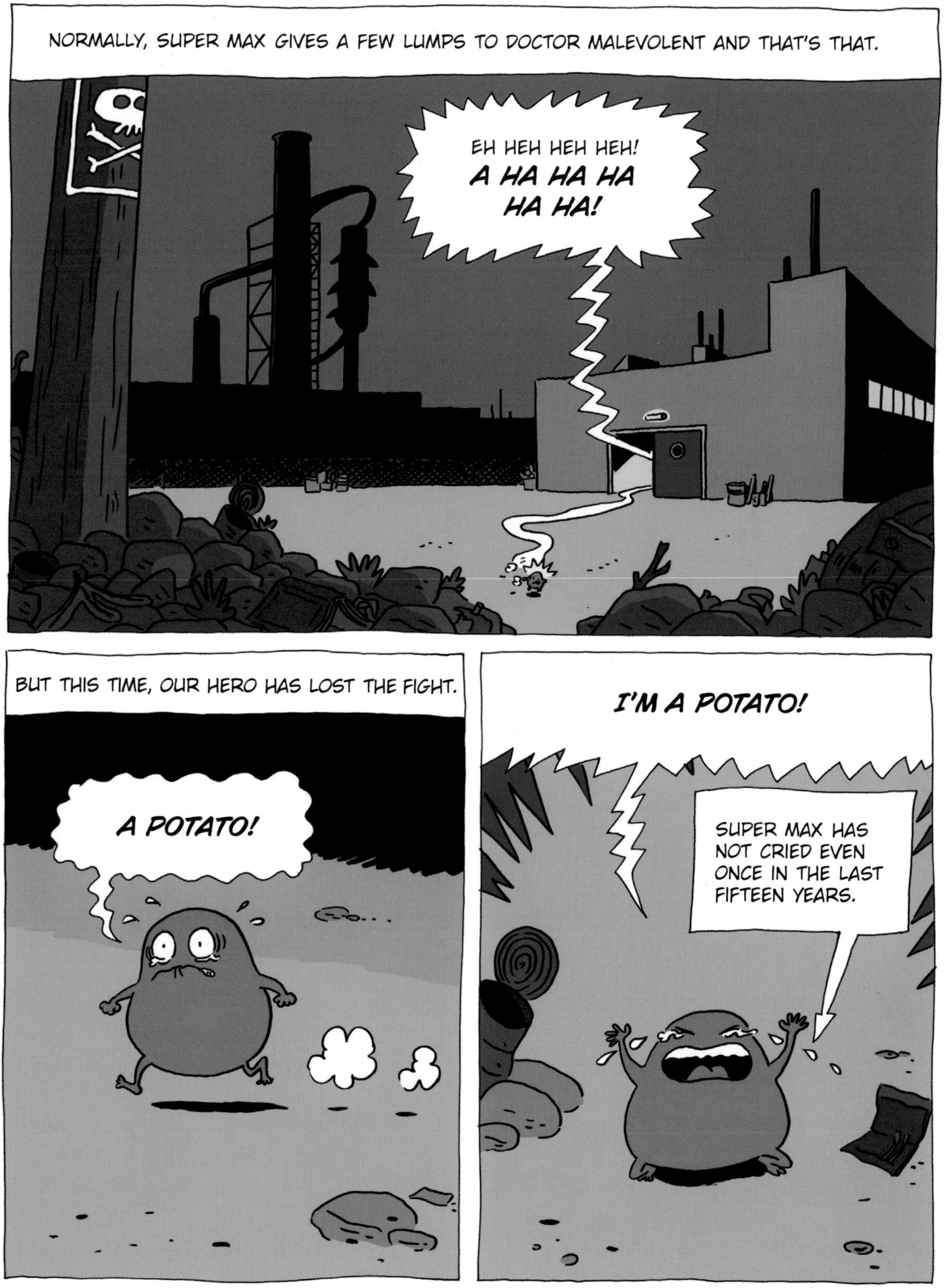
NORMALLY, SUPER MAX GIVES A FEW LUMPS TO DOCTOR MALEVOLENT AND THAT'S THAT.
EH HEH HEH HEH! A HA HA HA HA HA!
BUT THIS TIME, OUR HERO HAS LOST THE FIGHT.
A POTATO!
I'M A POTATO!
SUPER MAX HAS NOT CRIED EVEN ONCE IN THE LAST FIFTEEN YEARS.

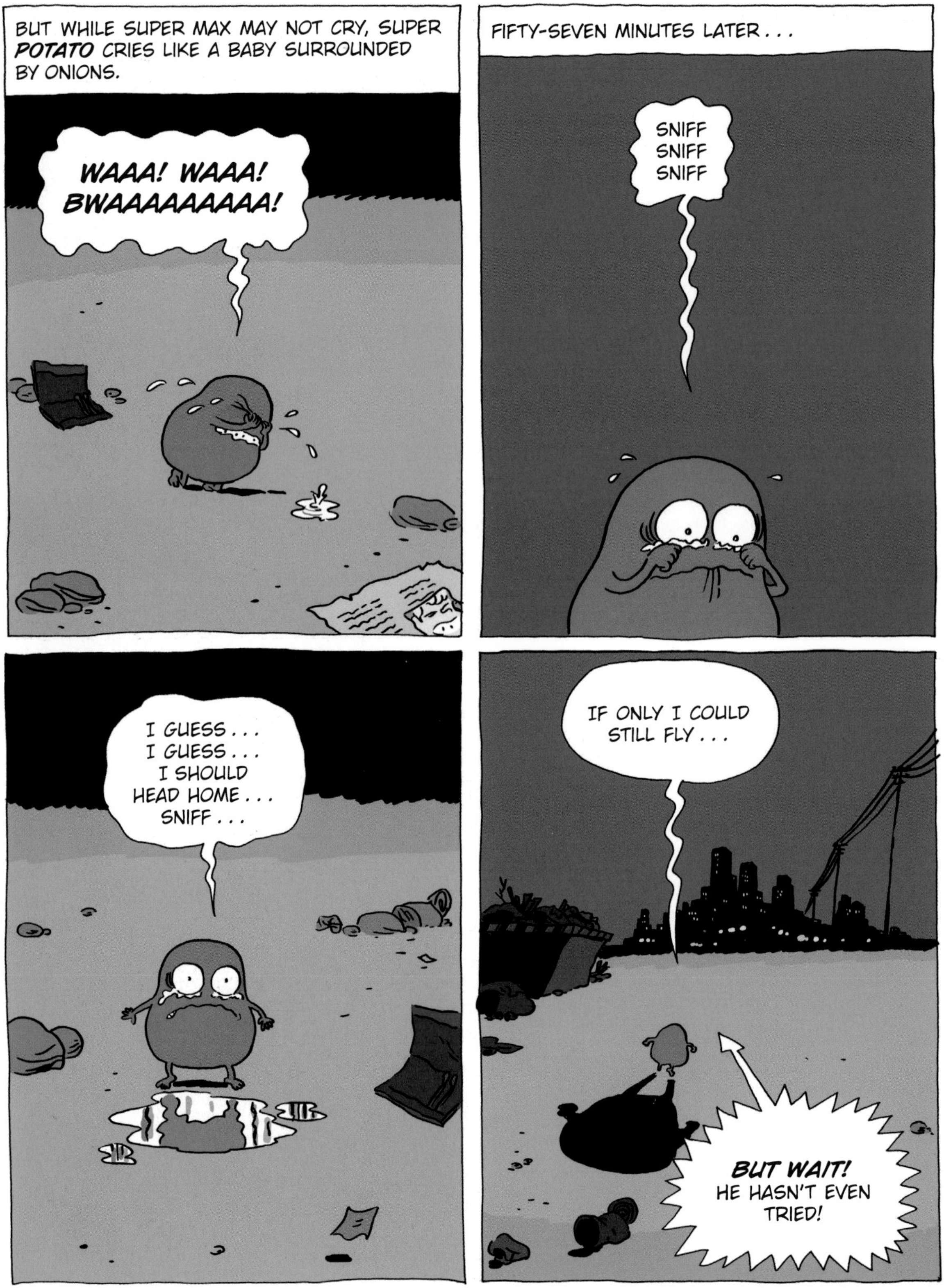
BUT WHILE SUPER MAX MAY NOT CRY, SUPER POTATO CRIES LIKE A BABY SURROUNDED BY ONIONS.
WAAA! WAAA! BWAAAAAAAAA!
FIFTY-SEVEN MINUTES LATER . . .
SNIFF SNIFF SNIFF
I GUESS . . . I GUESS . . . I SHOULD HEAD HOME . . . SNIFF . . .
IF ONLY I COULD STILL FLY . . .
BUT WAIT! HE HASN'T EVEN TRIED!

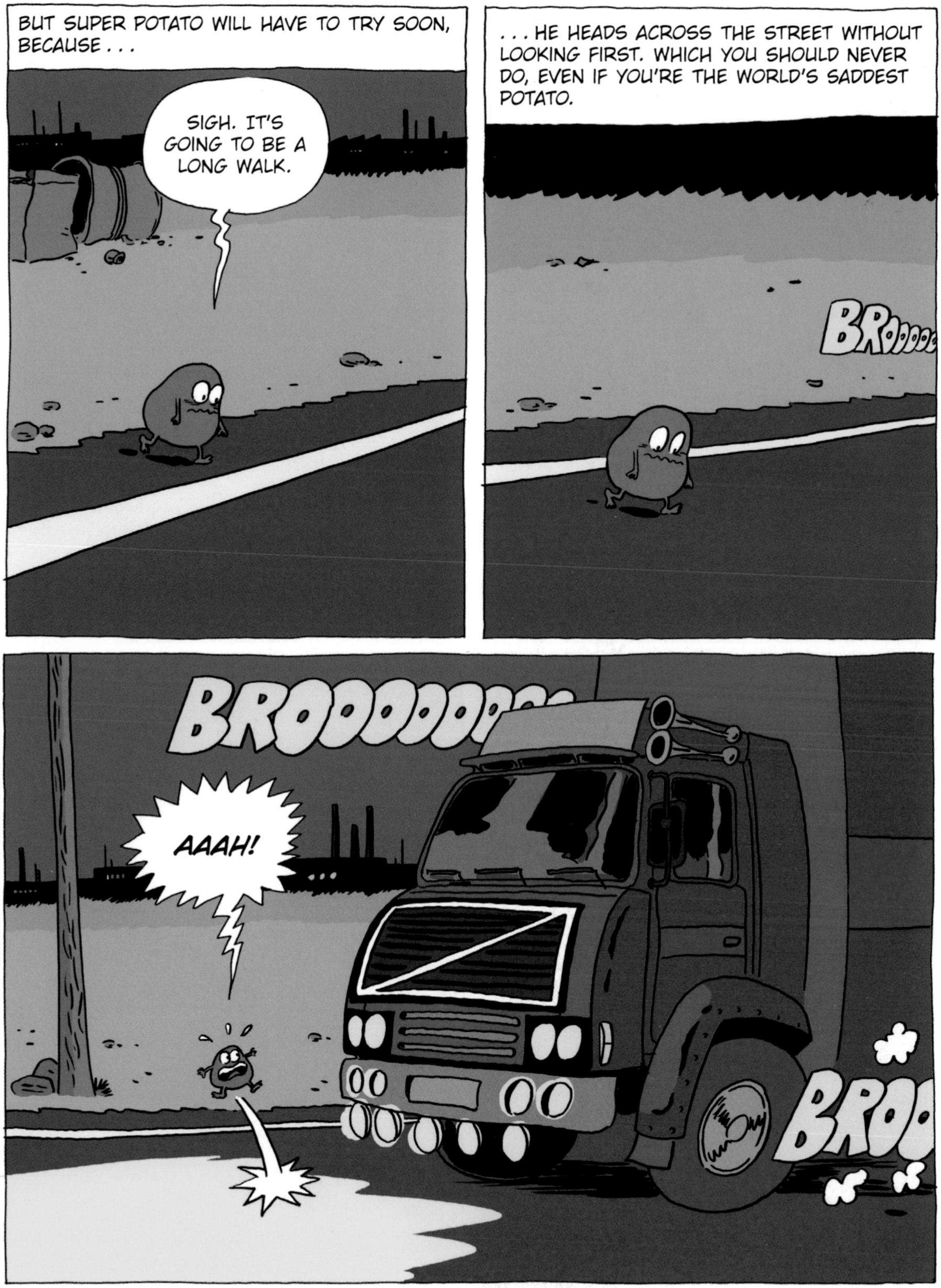

BUT SUPER POTATO WILL HAVE TO TRY SOON, BECAUSE . . .
SIGH. IT'S GOING TO BE A LONG WALK.
. . . HE HEADS ACROSS THE STREET WITHOUT LOOKING FIRST. WHICH YOU SHOULD NEVER DO, EVEN IF YOU'RE THE WORLD'S SADDEST POTATO.
BROOOOO
BROOOOOOO
AAAH!
BROO

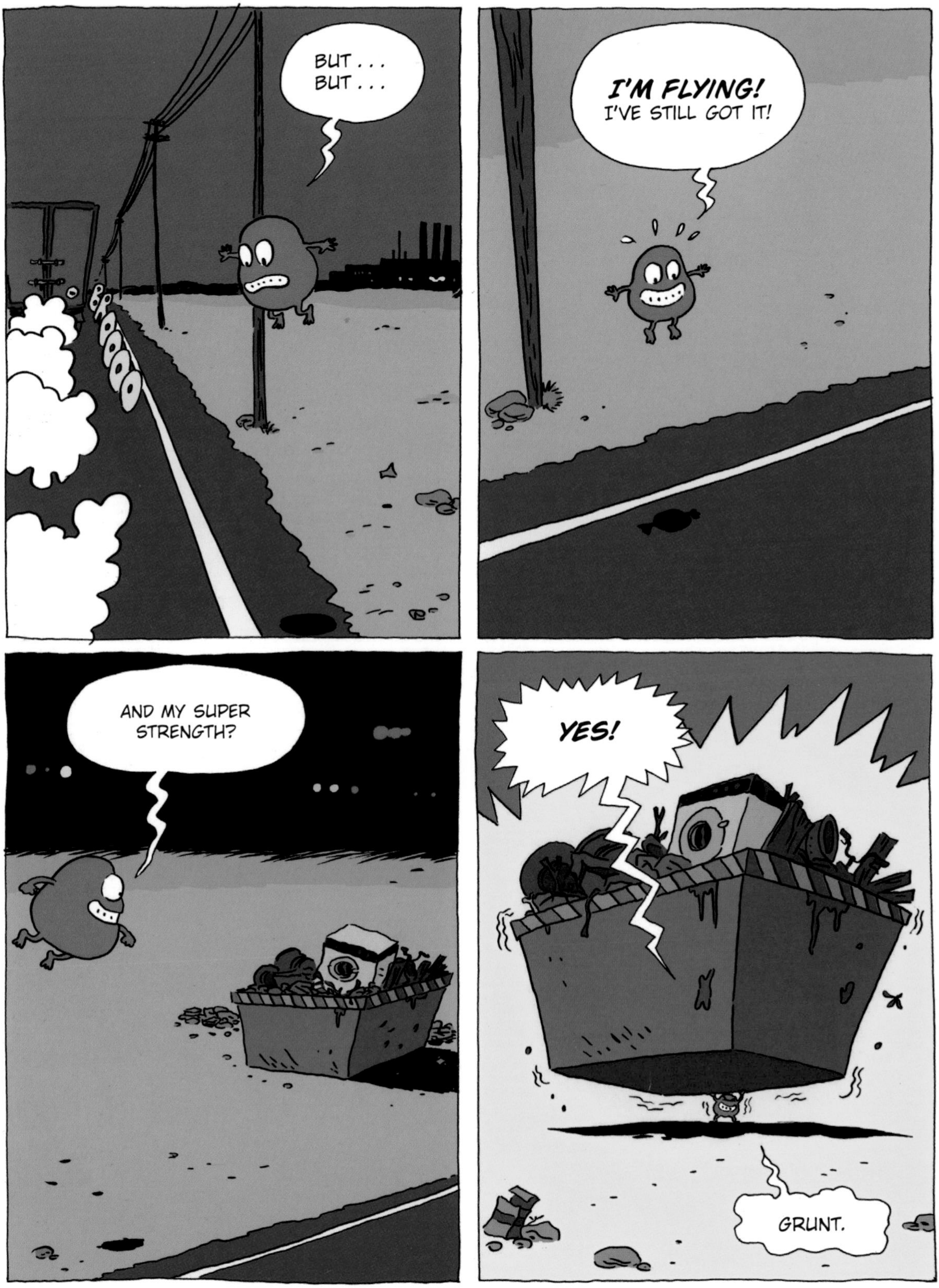
BUT . . .
BUT . . .
I'M FLYING!
I'VE STILL GOT IT!
AND MY SUPER STRENGTH?
YES!
GRUNT.

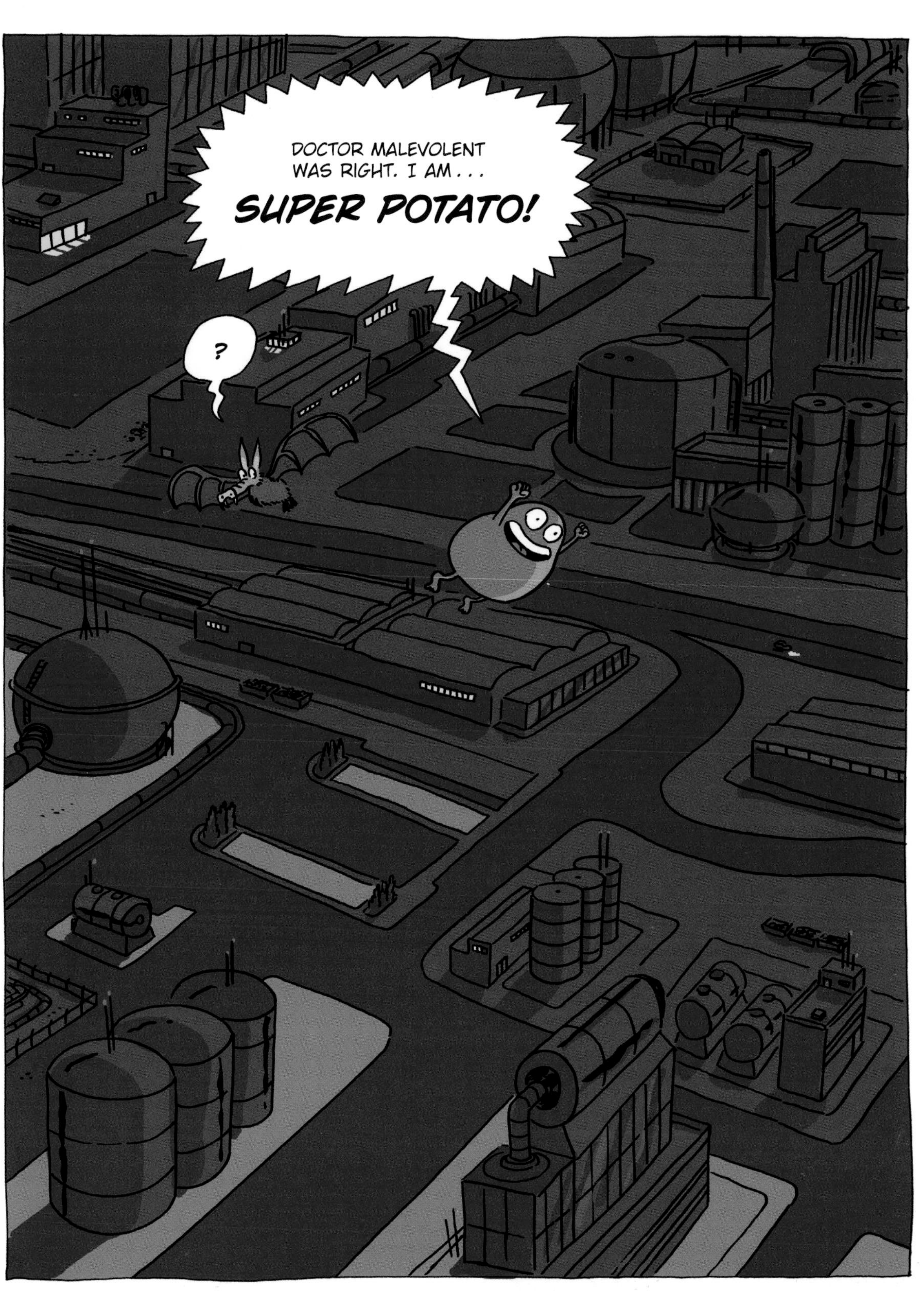
DOCTOR MALEVOLENT WAS RIGHT. I AM . . .
SUPER POTATO!
?

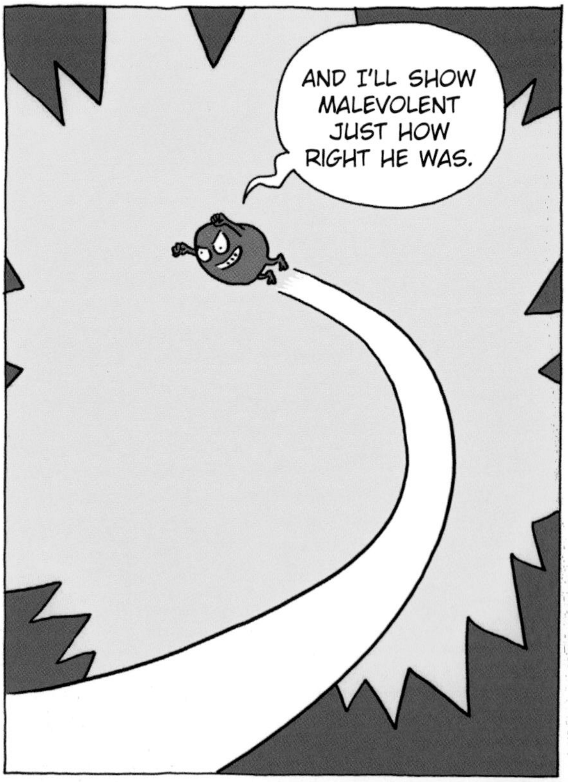
AND I'LL SHOW MALEVOLENT JUST HOW RIGHT HE WAS.

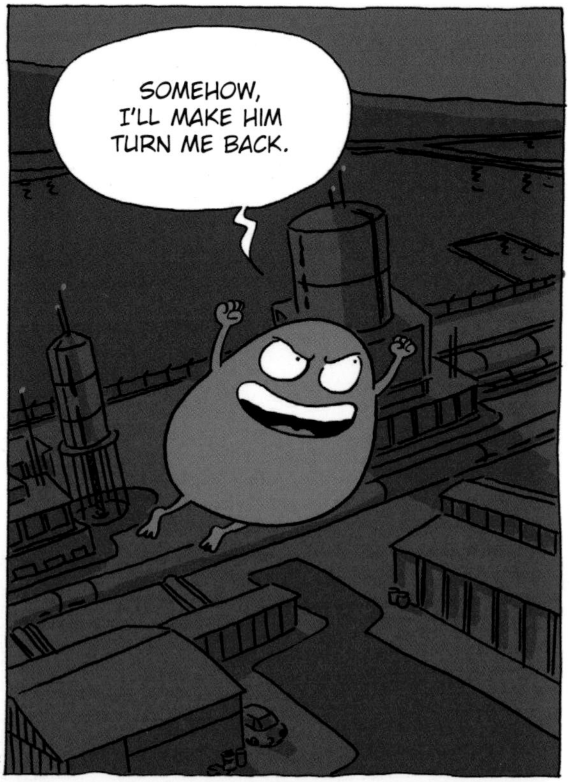
SOMEHOW, I'LL MAKE HIM TURN ME BACK.

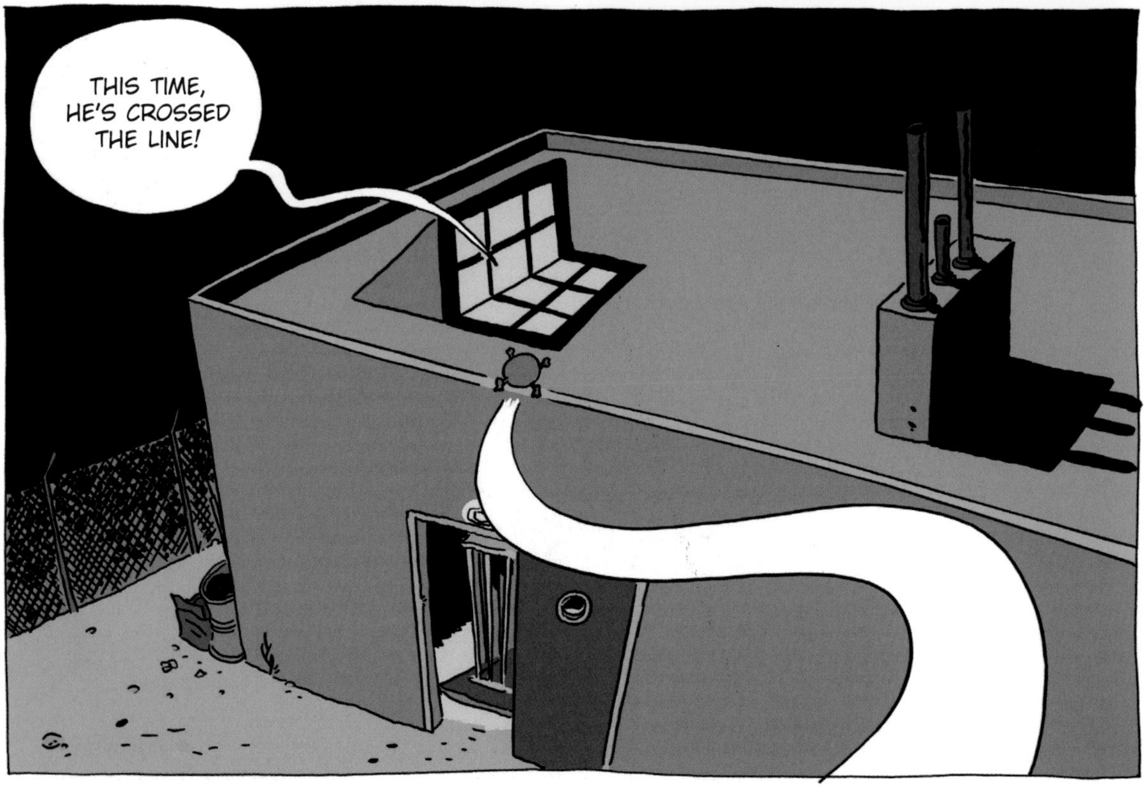
THIS TIME, HE'S CROSSED THE LINE!

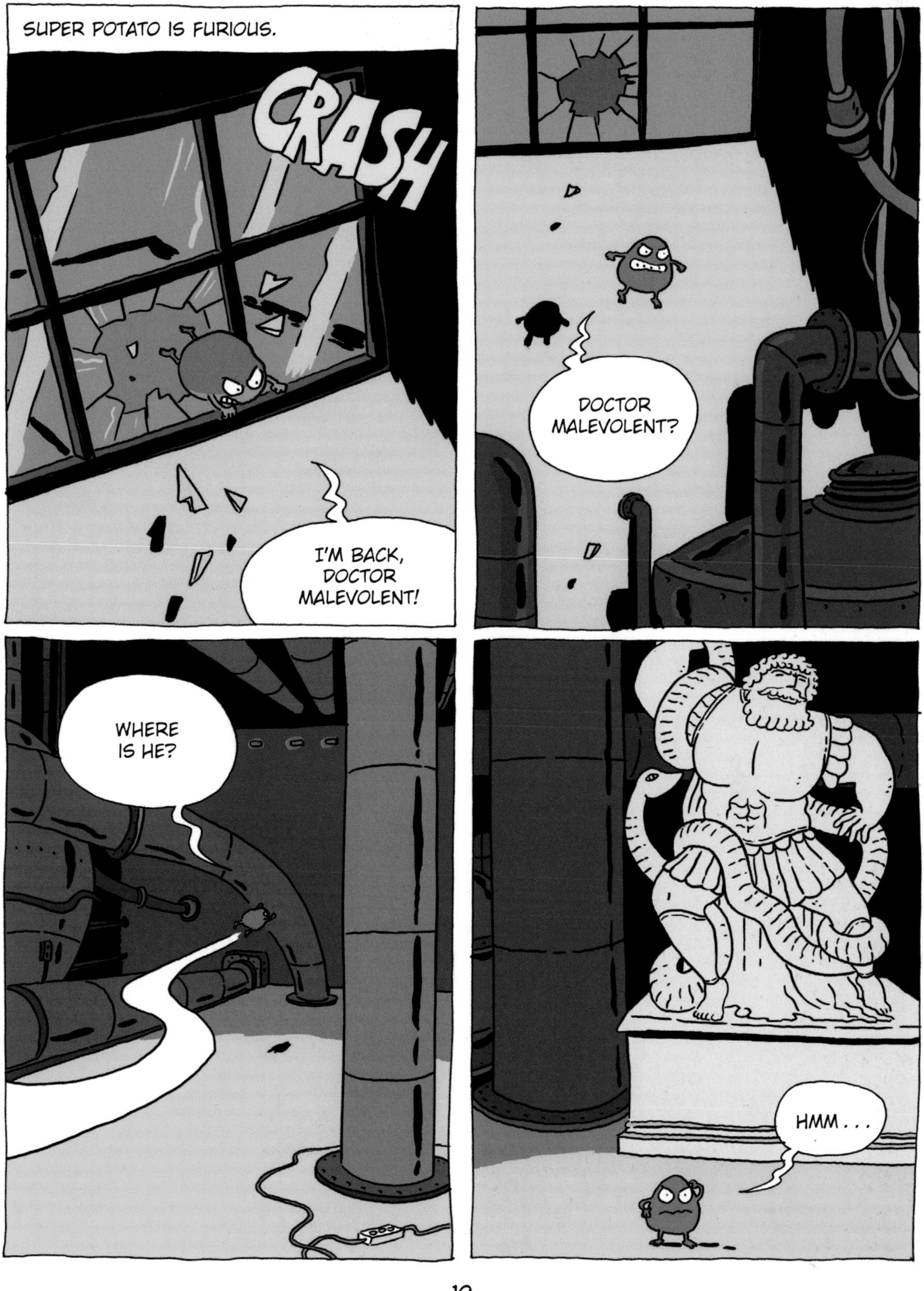
SUPER POTATO IS FURIOUS.
CRASH
I'M BACK, DOCTOR MALEVOLENT!
DOCTOR MALEVOLENT?
WHERE IS HE?
HMM . . .

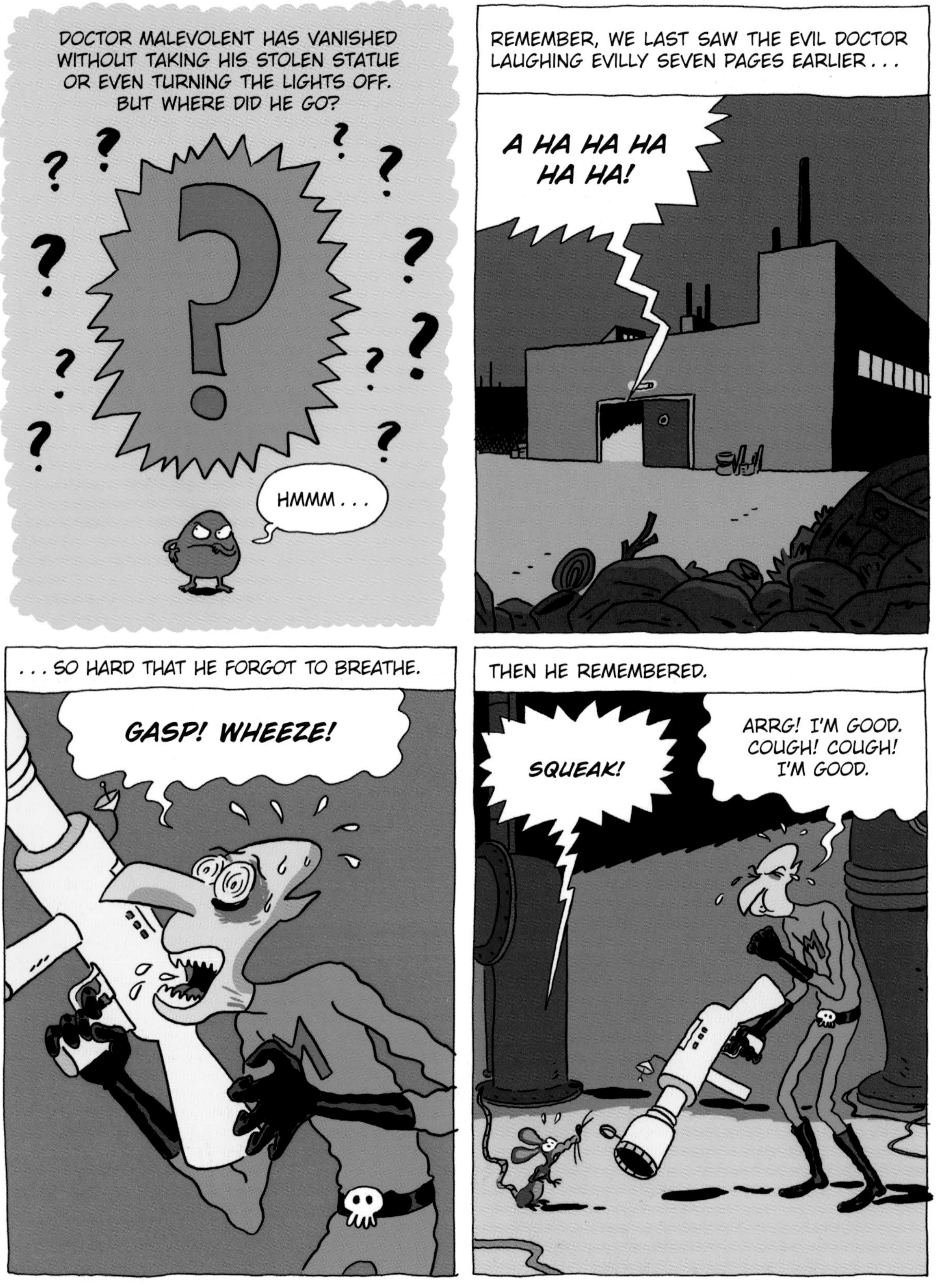
DOCTOR MALEVOLENT HAS VANISHED WITHOUT TAKING HIS STOLEN STATUE OR EVEN TURNING THE LIGHTS OFF. BUT WHERE DID HE GO?
HMMM . . .
REMEMBER, WE LAST SAW THE EVIL DOCTOR LAUGHING EVILLY SEVEN PAGES EARLIER . . .
A HA HA HA HA HA!
. . . SO HARD THAT HE FORGOT TO BREATHE.
GASP! WHEEZE!
THEN HE REMEMBERED.
SQUEAK!
ARRG! I'M GOOD. COUGH! COUGH! I'M GOOD.

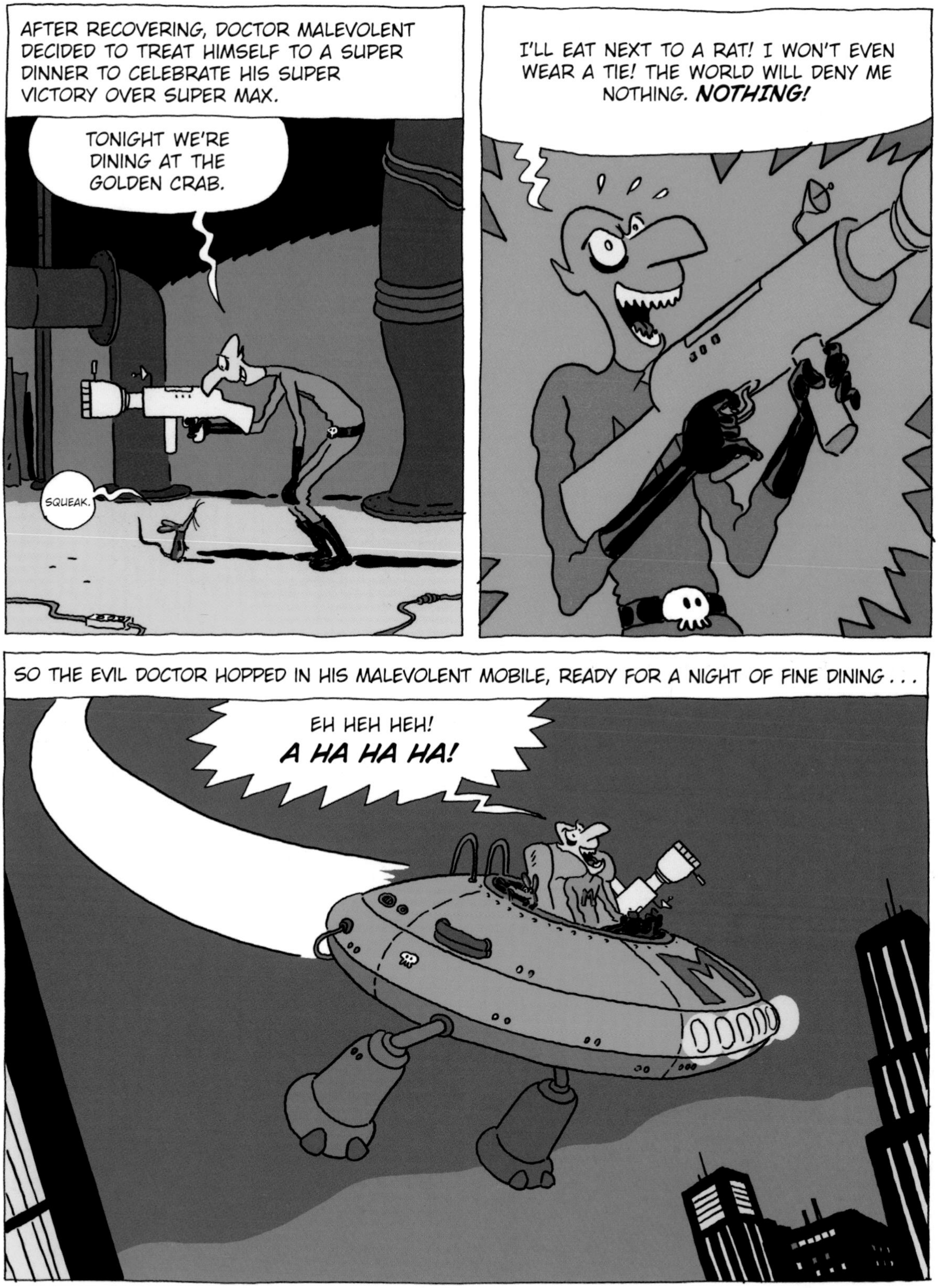
AFTER RECOVERING, DOCTOR MALEVOLENT DECIDED TO TREAT HIMSELF TO A SUPER DINNER TO CELEBRATE HIS SUPER VICTORY OVER SUPER MAX.
TONIGHT WE'RE DINING AT THE GOLDEN CRAB.
SQUEAK.
I'LL EAT NEXT TO A RAT! I WON'T EVEN WEAR A TIE! THE WORLD WILL DENY ME NOTHING. NOTHING!
SO THE EVIL DOCTOR HOPPED IN HIS MALEVOLENT MOBILE, READY FOR A NIGHT OF FINE DINING . . .
EH HEH HEH!
A HA HA HA!

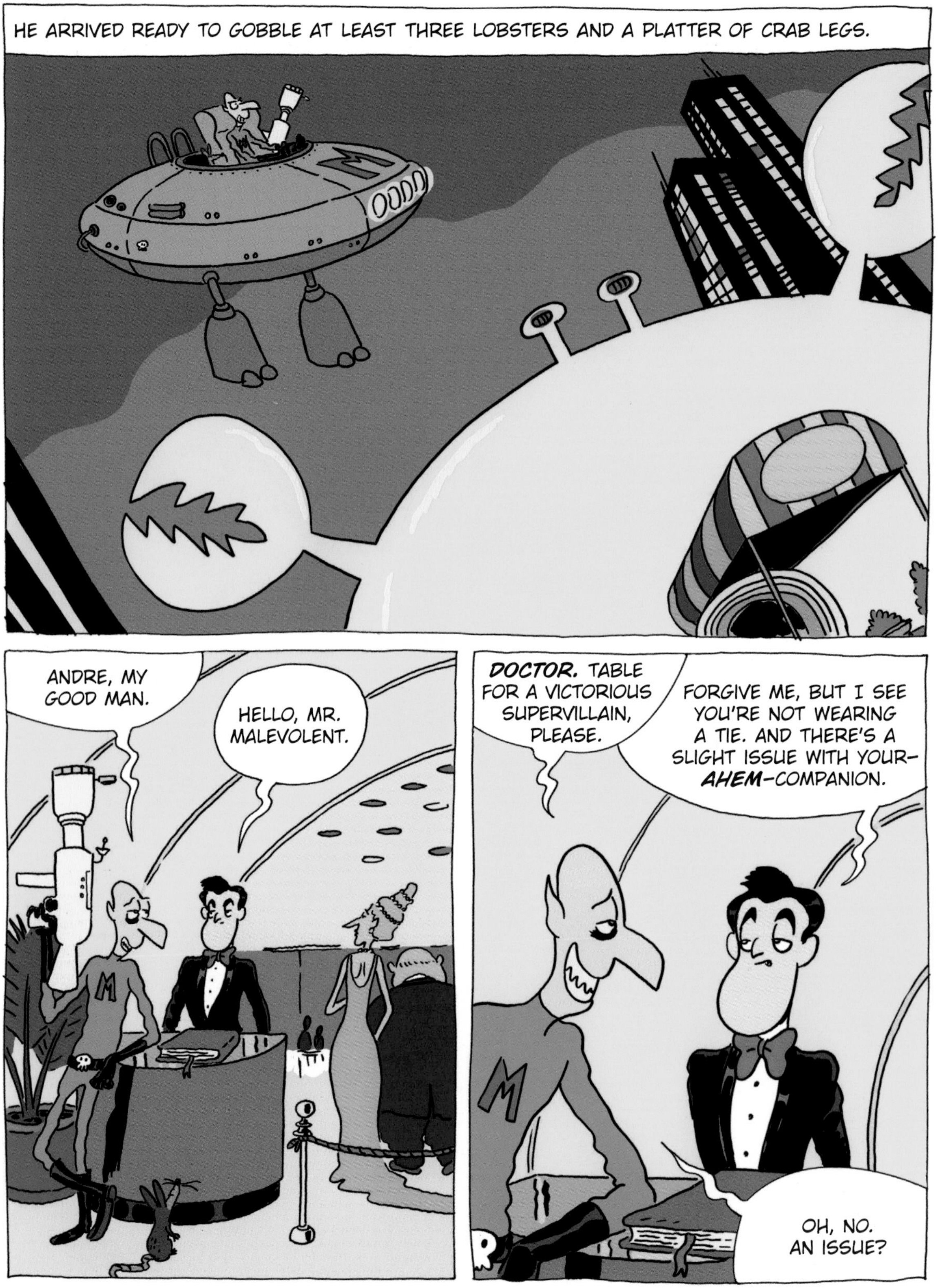
HE ARRIVED READY TO GOBBLE AT LEAST THREE LOBSTERS AND A PLATTER OF CRAB LEGS.
ANDRE, MY GOOD MAN.
HELLO, MR. MALEVOLENT.
DOCTOR. TABLE FOR A VICTORIOUS SUPERVILLAIN, PLEASE.
FORGIVE ME, BUT I SEE YOU'RE NOT WEARING A TIE. AND THERE'S A SLIGHT ISSUE WITH YOUR- AHEM-COMPANION.
OH, NO. AN ISSUE?

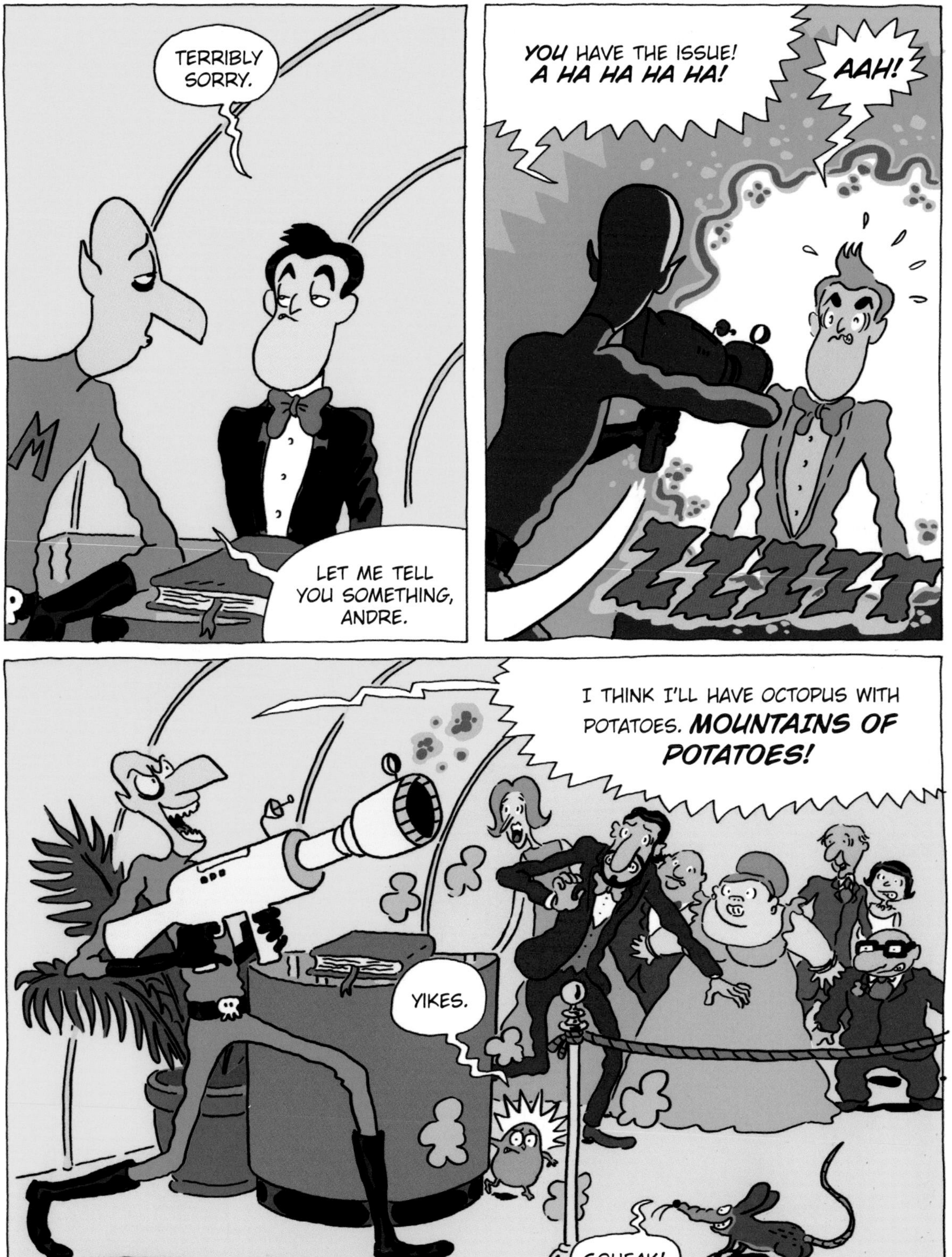
TERRIBLY SORRY.
LET ME TELL YOU SOMETHING, ANDRE.
YOU HAVE THE ISSUE! A HA HA HA HA!
AAH!
ZZZZZT
I THINK I'LL HAVE OCTOPUS WITH POTATOES. MOUNTAINS OF POTATOES!
YIKES.
SQUEAK!

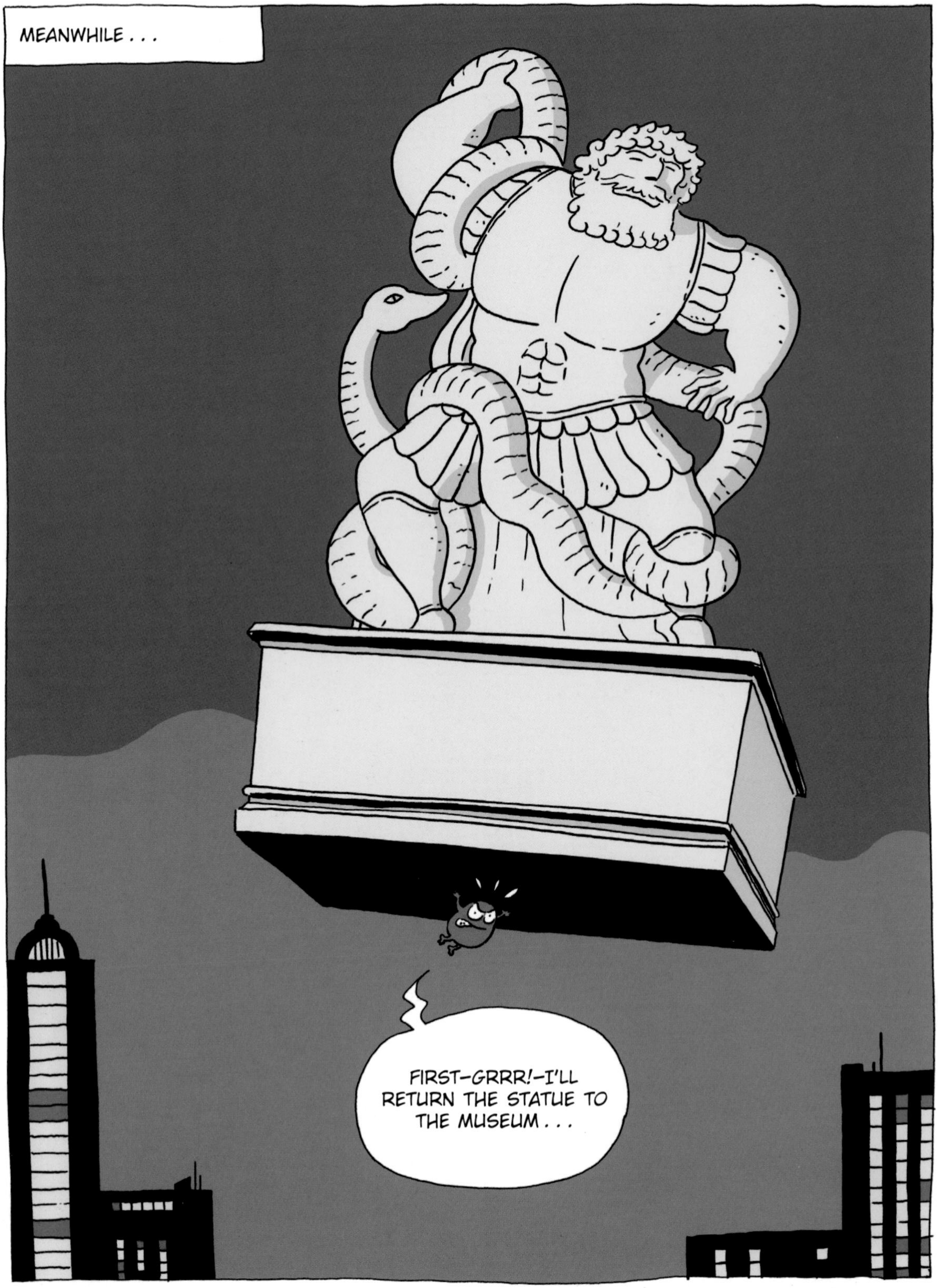
MEANWHILE . . .
FIRST—GRRR!—I'LL RETURN THE STATUE TO THE MUSEUM . . .

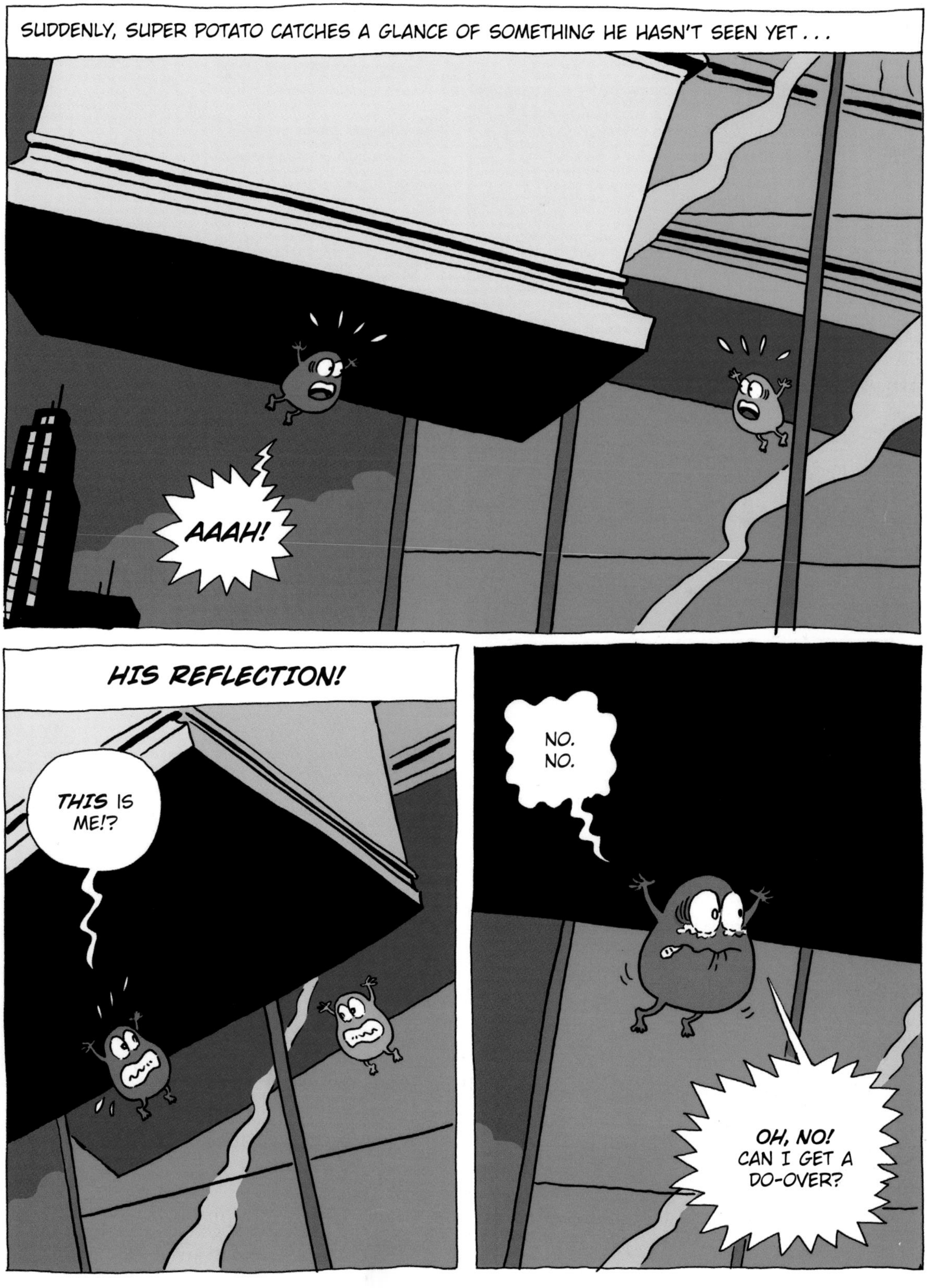
SUDDENLY, SUPER POTATO CATCHES A GLANCE OF SOMETHING HE HASN'T SEEN YET . . .
AAAH!
HIS REFLECTION!
THIS IS ME!?
NO. NO.
OH, NO! CAN I GET A DO-OVER?

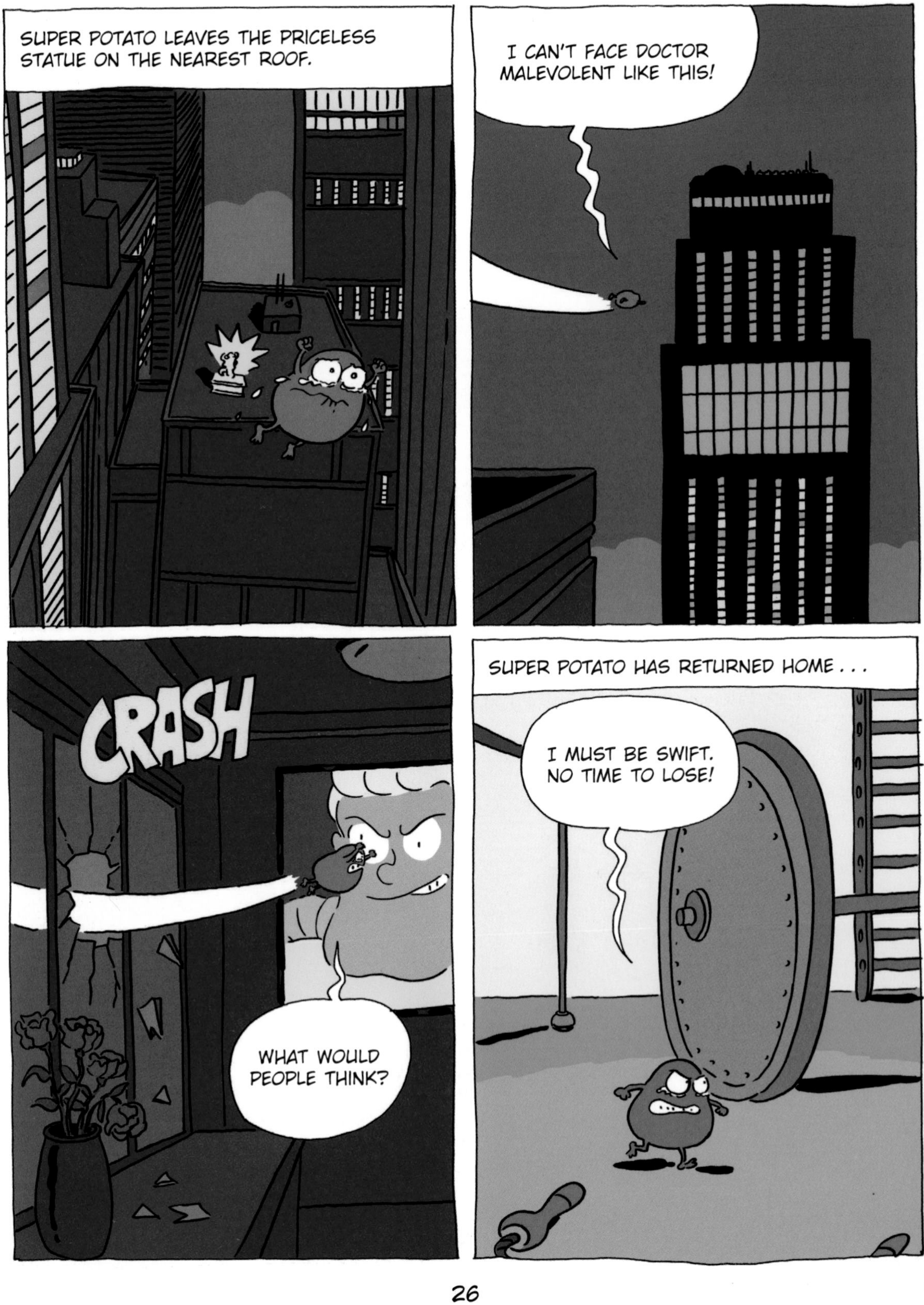
SUPER POTATO LEAVES THE PRICELESS STATUE ON THE NEAREST ROOF.
I CAN'T FACE DOCTOR MALEVOLENT LIKE THIS!
CRASH
WHAT WOULD PEOPLE THINK?
SUPER POTATO HAS RETURNED HOME . . .
I MUST BE SWIFT. NO TIME TO LOSE!

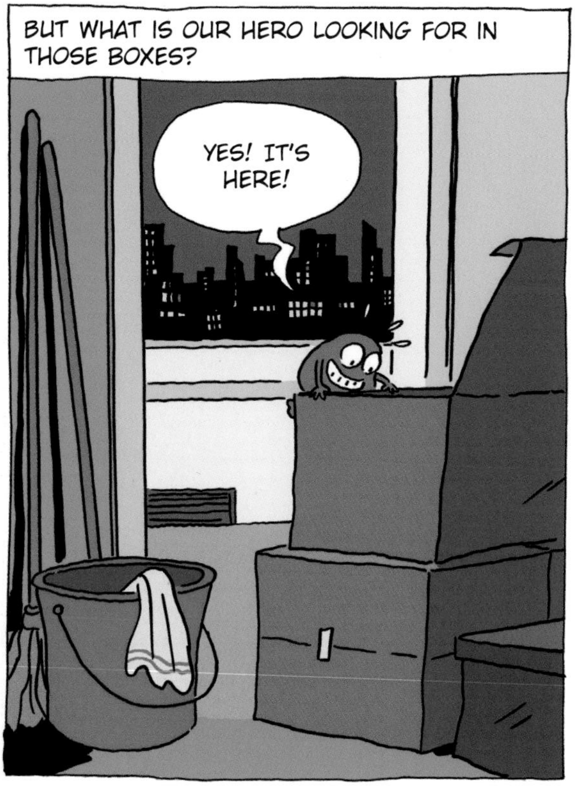
BUT WHAT IS OUR HERO LOOKING FOR IN THOSE BOXES?
YES! IT'S HERE!

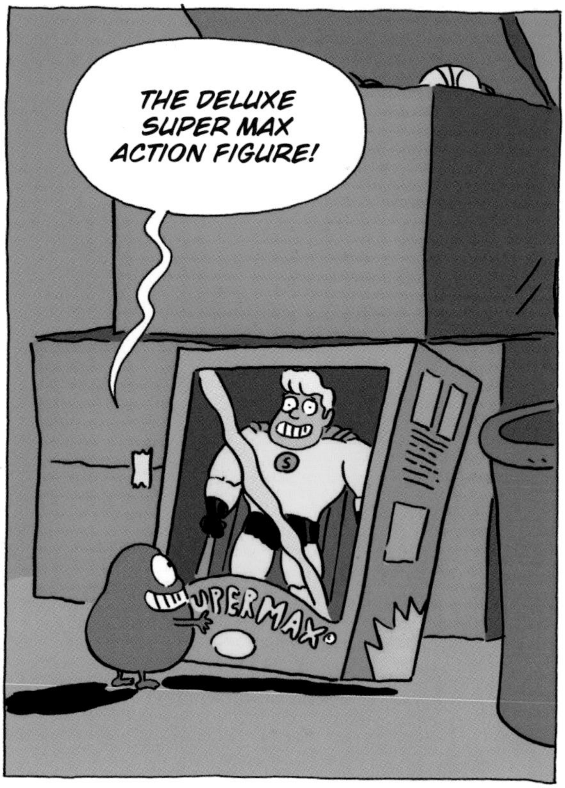
THE DELUXE SUPER MAX ACTION FIGURE!
SUPERMAX

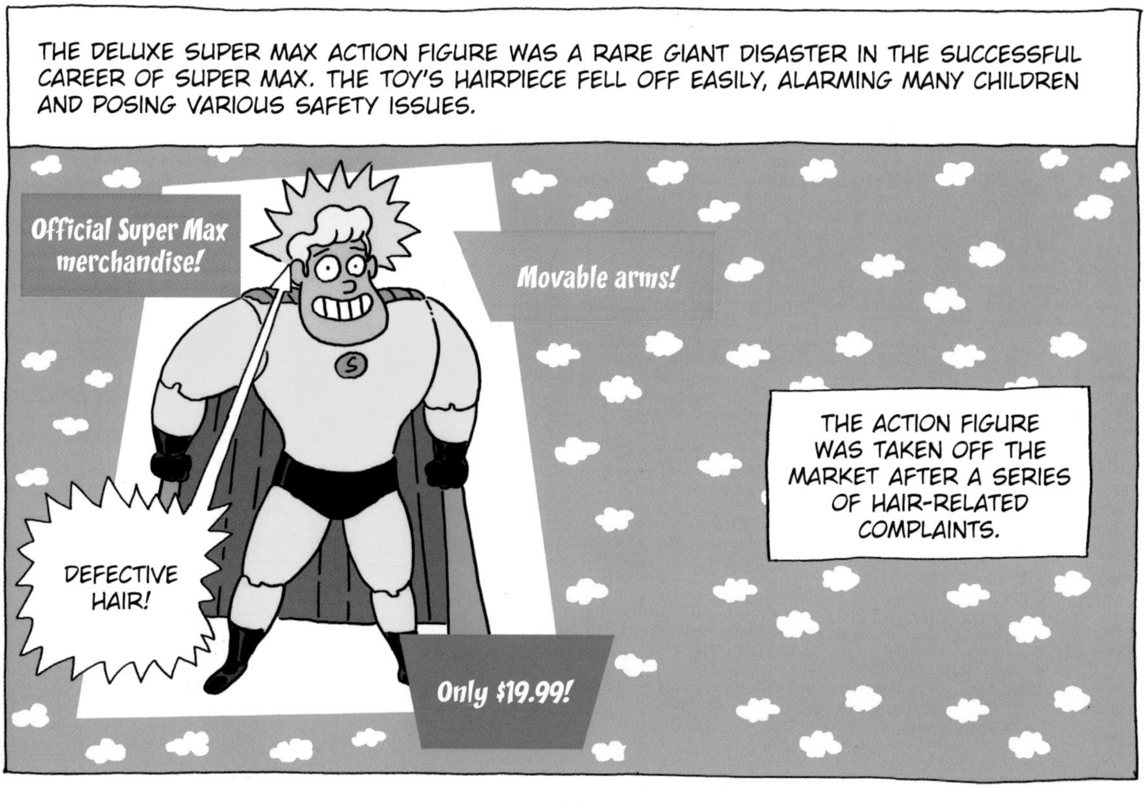
THE DELUXE SUPER MAX ACTION FIGURE WAS A RARE GIANT DISASTER IN THE SUCCESSFUL CAREER OF SUPER MAX. THE TOY'S HAIRPIECE FELL OFF EASILY, ALARMING MANY CHILDREN AND POSING VARIOUS SAFETY ISSUES.
Official Super Max merchandise!
Movable arms!
THE ACTION FIGURE WAS TAKEN OFF THE MARKET AFTER A SERIES OF HAIR-RELATED COMPLAINTS.
DEFECTIVE HAIR!
Only $19.99!

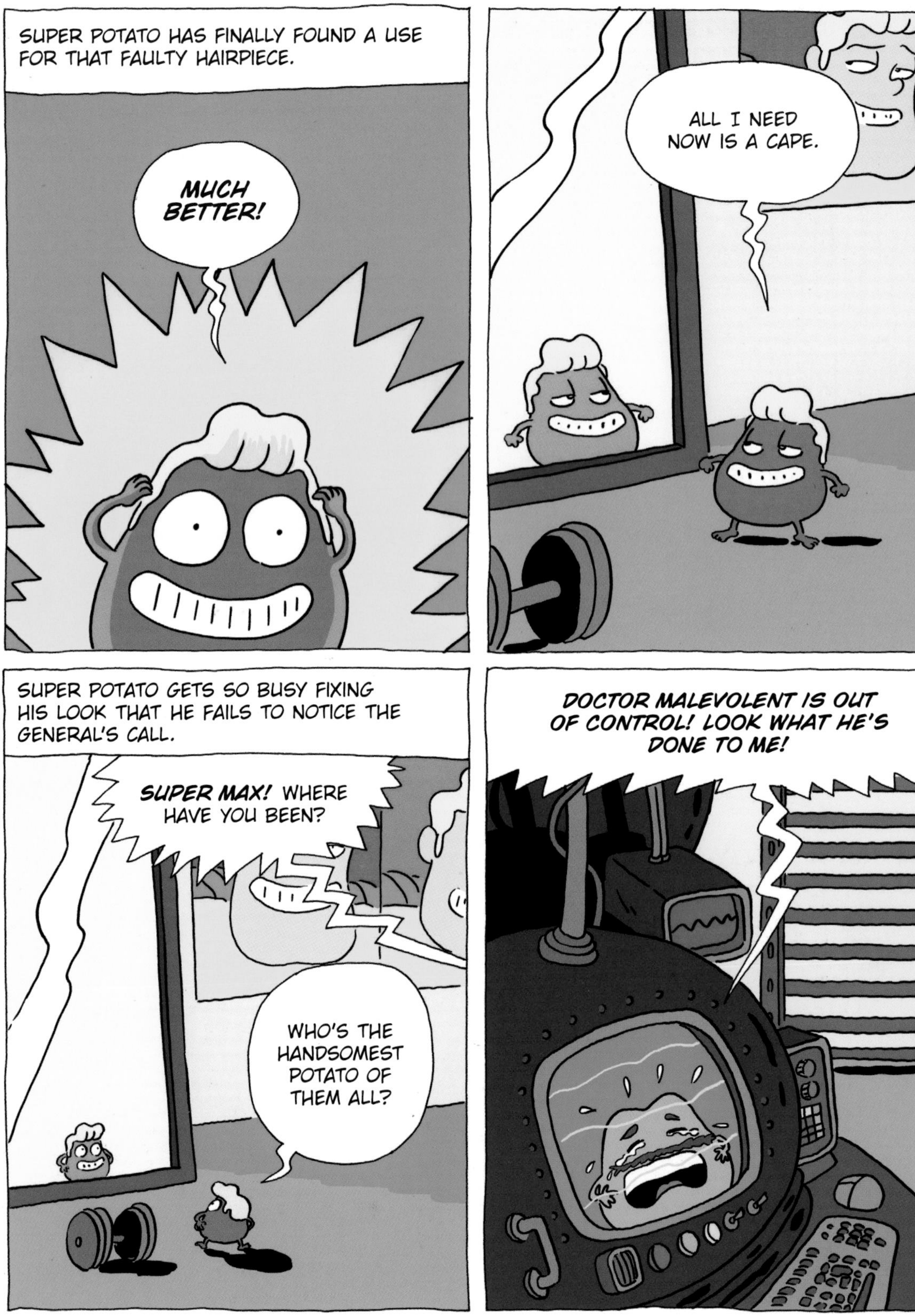
SUPER POTATO HAS FINALLY FOUND A USE FOR THAT FAULTY HAIRPIECE.
MUCH BETTER!
ALL I NEED NOW IS A CAPE.
SUPER POTATO GETS SO BUSY FIXING HIS LOOK THAT HE FAILS TO NOTICE THE GENERAL'S CALL.
SUPER MAX! WHERE HAVE YOU BEEN?
WHO'S THE HANDSOMEST POTATO OF THEM ALL?
DOCTOR MALEVOLENT IS OUT OF CONTROL! LOOK WHAT HE'S DONE TO ME!

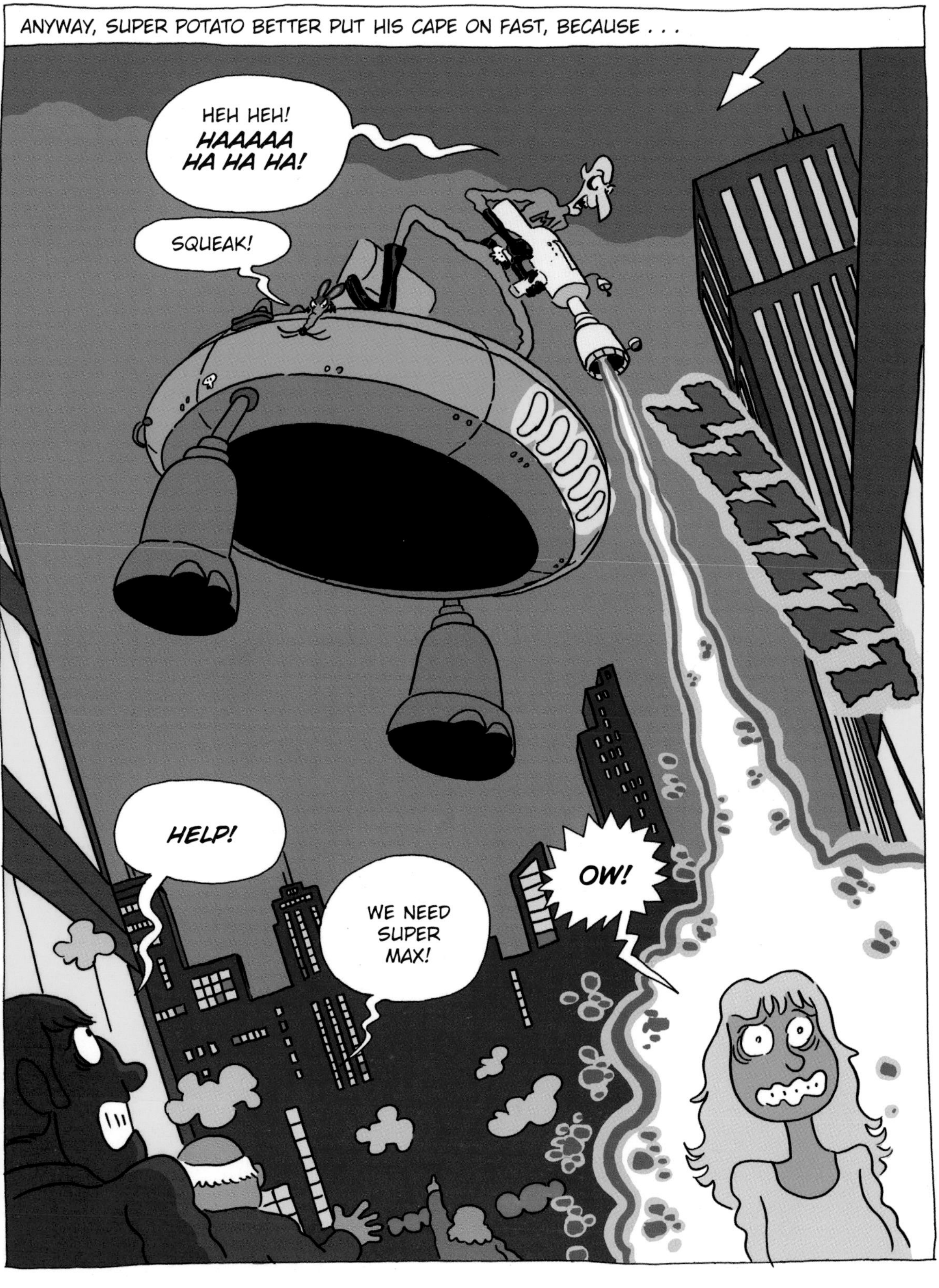
ANYWAY, SUPER POTATO BETTER PUT HIS CAPE ON FAST, BECAUSE . . .
HEH HEH! HAAAAA HA HA HA!
SQUEAK!
HELP!
WE NEED SUPER MAX!
OW!

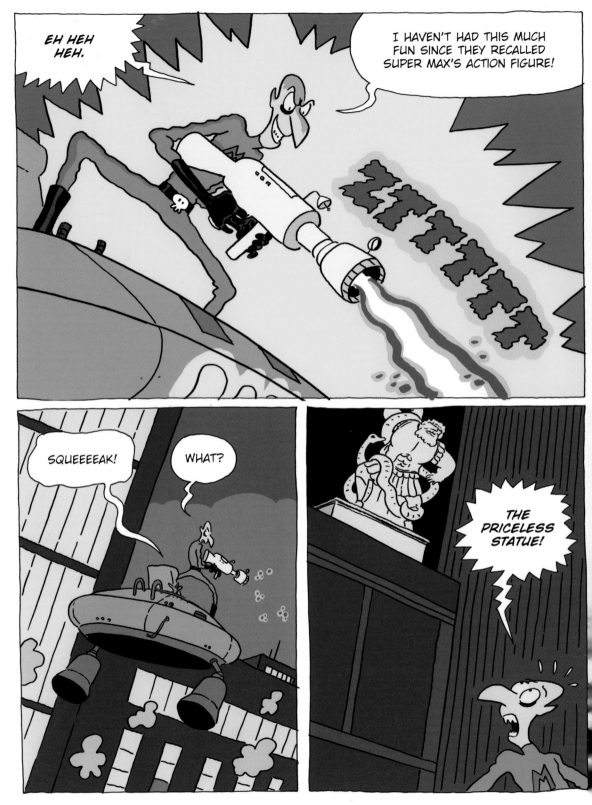

EH HEH HEH.

I HAVEN'T HAD THIS MUCH FUN SINCE THEY RECALLED SUPER MAX'S ACTION FIGURE!

SQUEEEEAK!

WHAT?

THE PRICELESS STATUE!

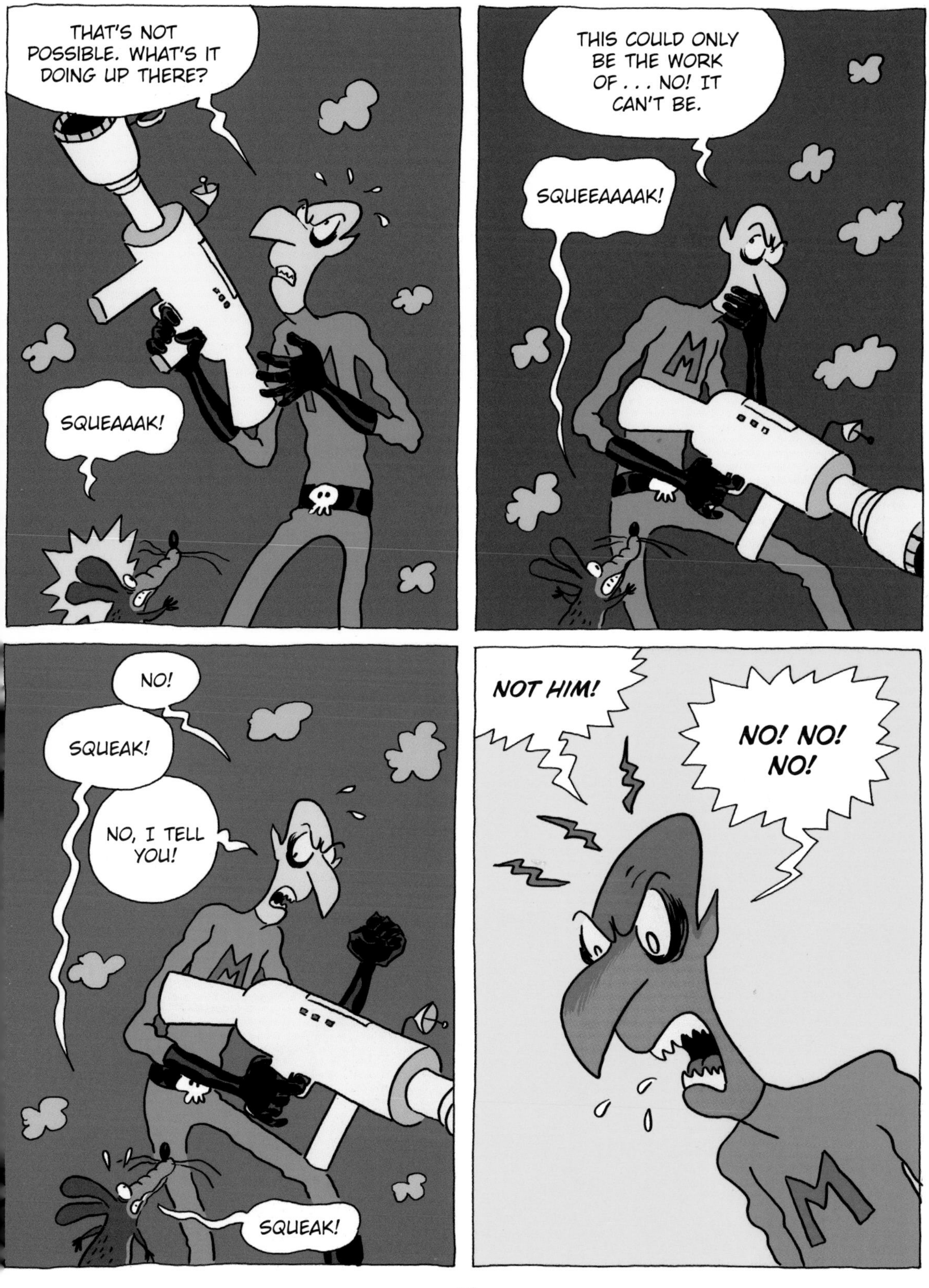
THAT'S NOT POSSIBLE. WHAT'S IT DOING UP THERE?
SQUEAAAK!
THIS COULD ONLY BE THE WORK OF . . . NO! IT CAN'T BE.
SQUEEAAAAK!
NO!
SQUEAK!
NO, I TELL YOU!
SQUEAK!
NOT HIM!
NO! NO! NO!

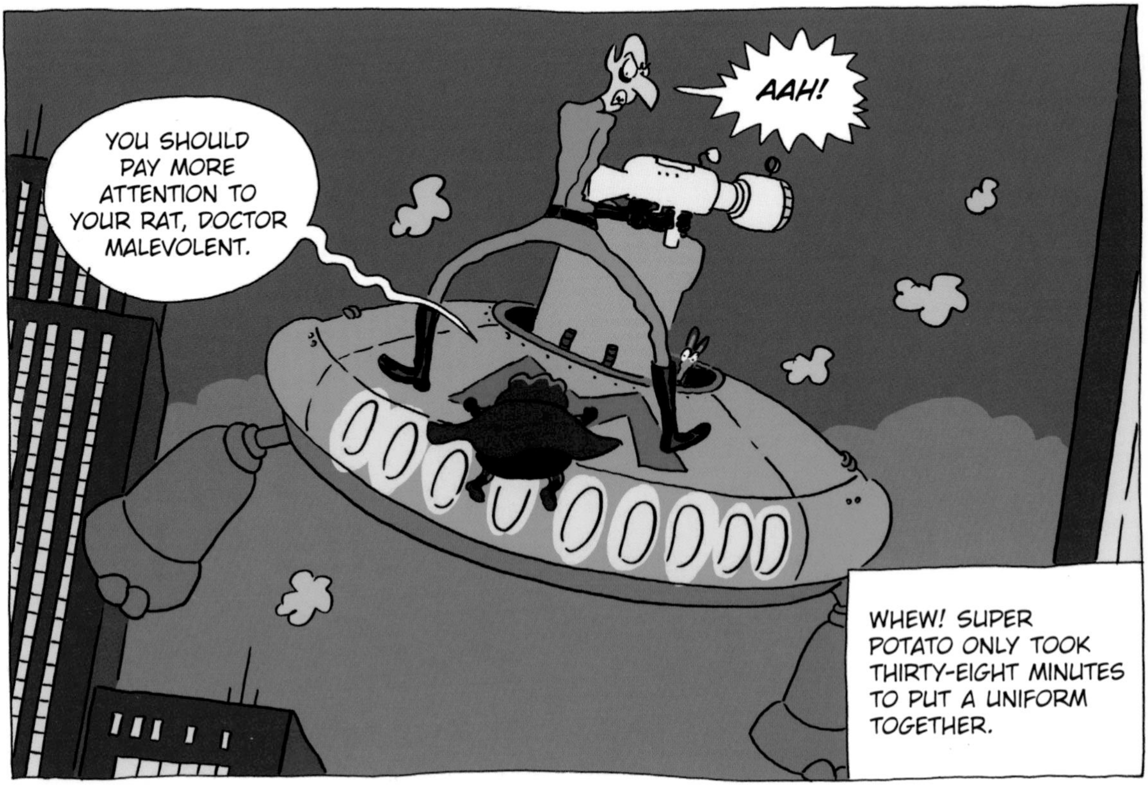
YOU SHOULD PAY MORE ATTENTION TO YOUR RAT, DOCTOR MALEVOLENT.
AAH!
WHEW! SUPER POTATO ONLY TOOK THIRTY-EIGHT MINUTES TO PUT A UNIFORM TOGETHER.

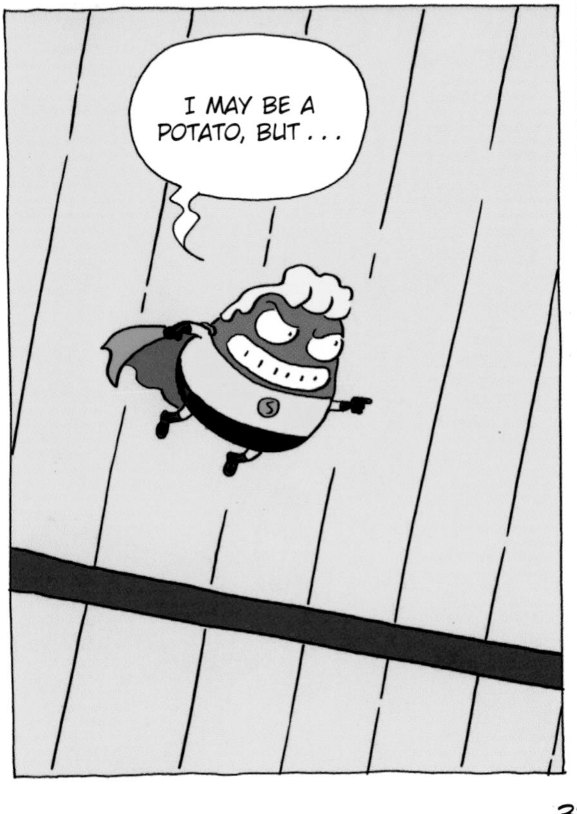
I MAY BE A POTATO, BUT . . .

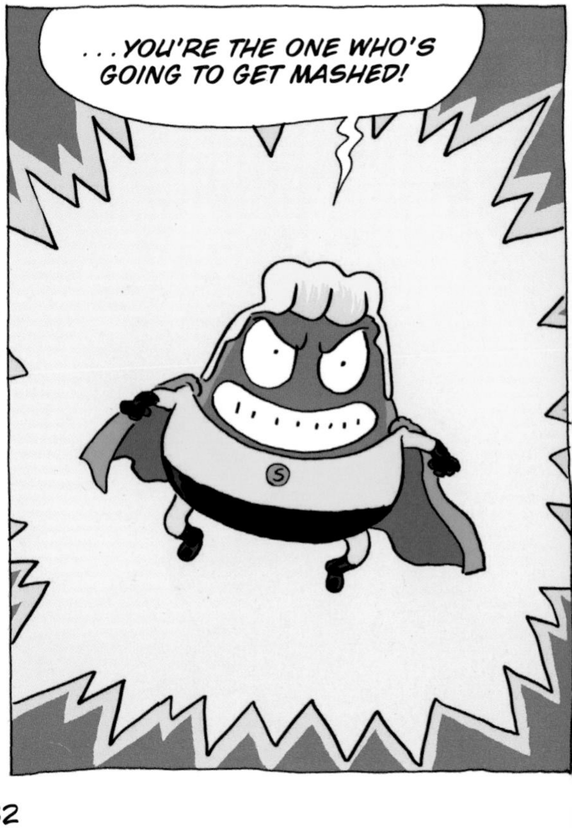
. . . YOU'RE THE ONE WHO'S GOING TO GET MASHED!

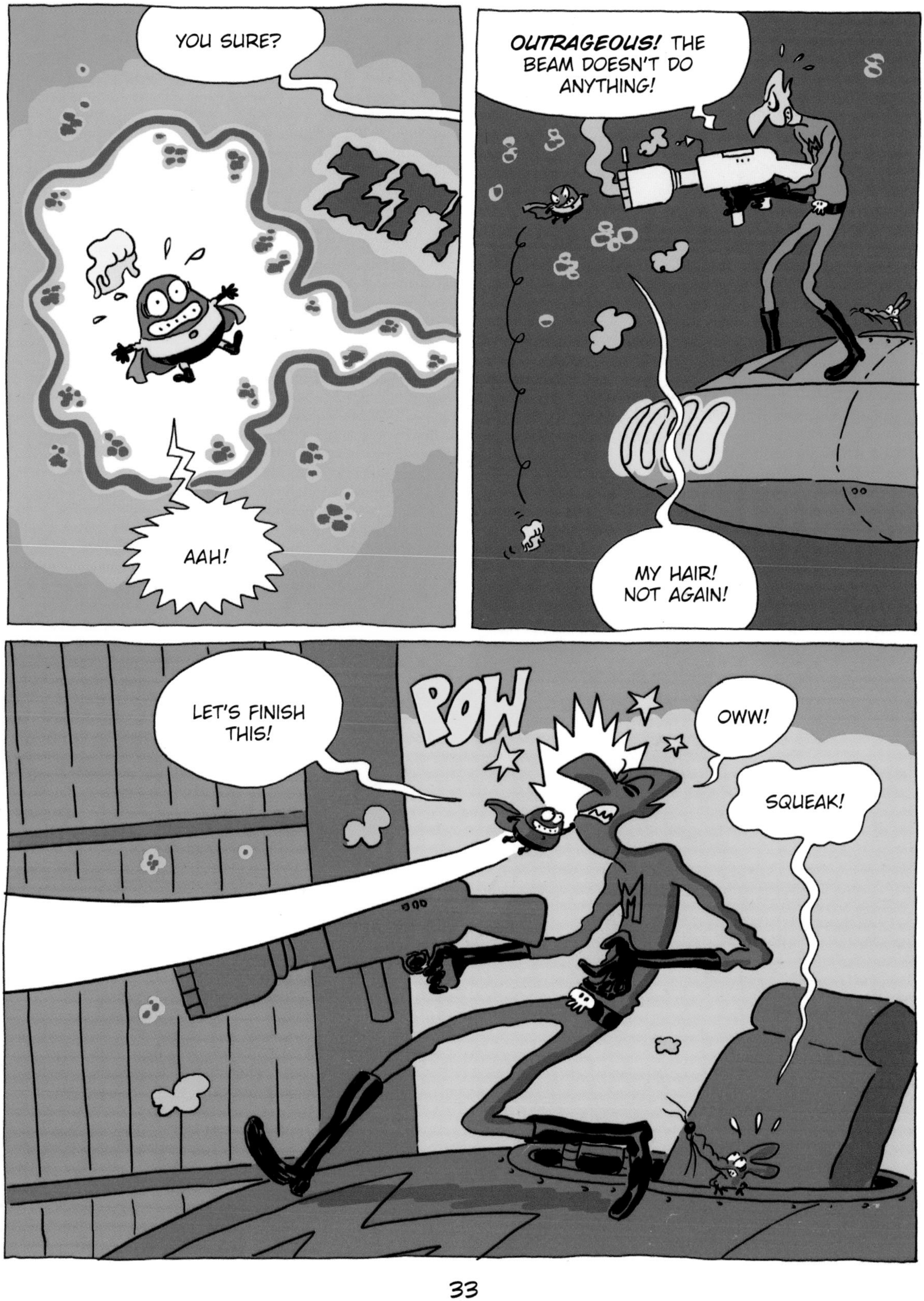
YOU SURE?
AAH!
OUTRAGEOUS! THE BEAM DOESN'T DO ANYTHING!
MY HAIR! NOT AGAIN!
LET'S FINISH THIS!
POW
OWW!
SQUEAK!

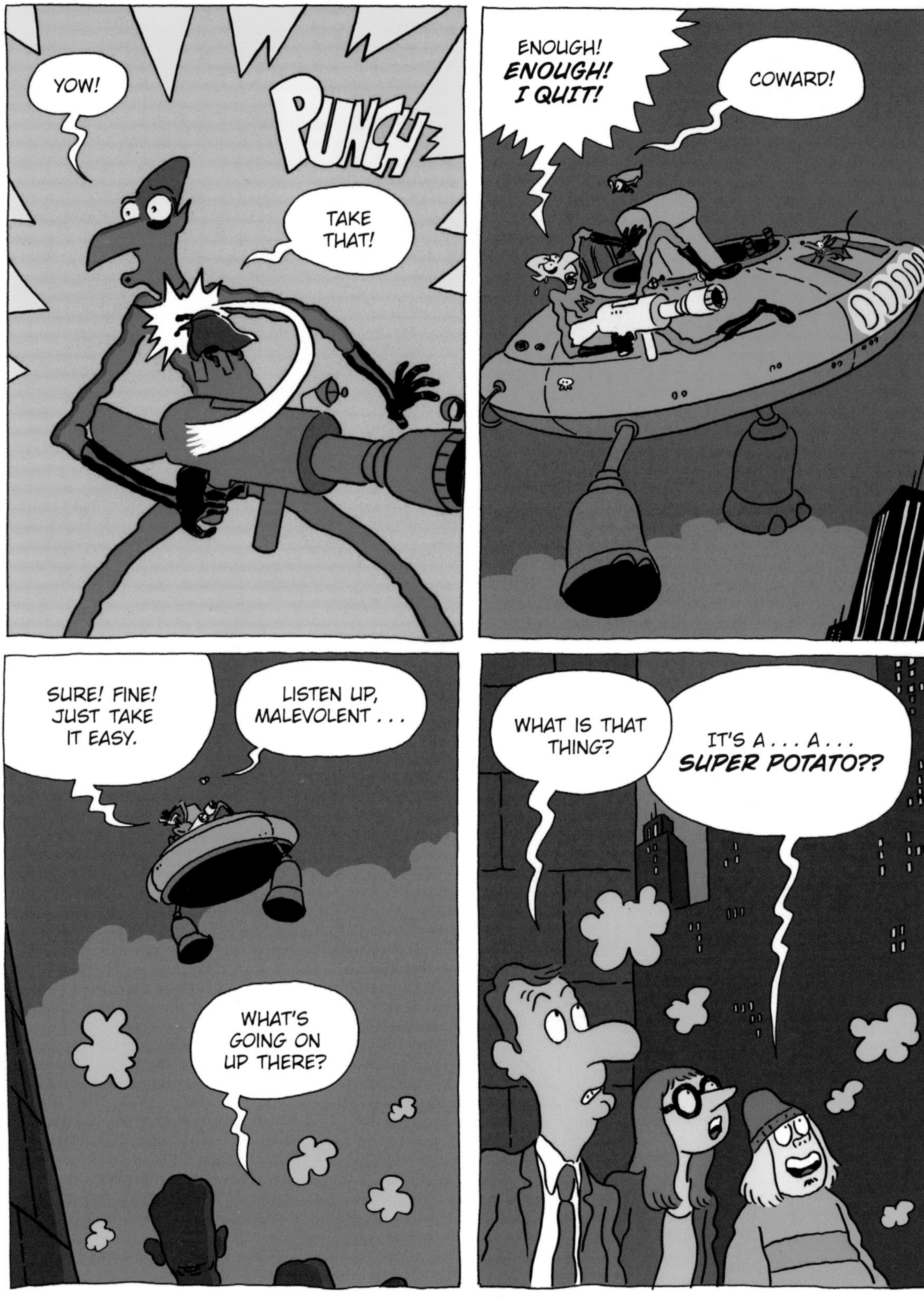
YOW!
PUNCH
TAKE THAT!
ENOUGH! ENOUGH! I QUIT!
COWARD!
SURE! FINE! JUST TAKE IT EASY.
LISTEN UP, MALEVOLENT . . .
WHAT'S GOING ON UP THERE?
WHAT IS THAT THING?
IT'S A . . . A . . . SUPER POTATO??

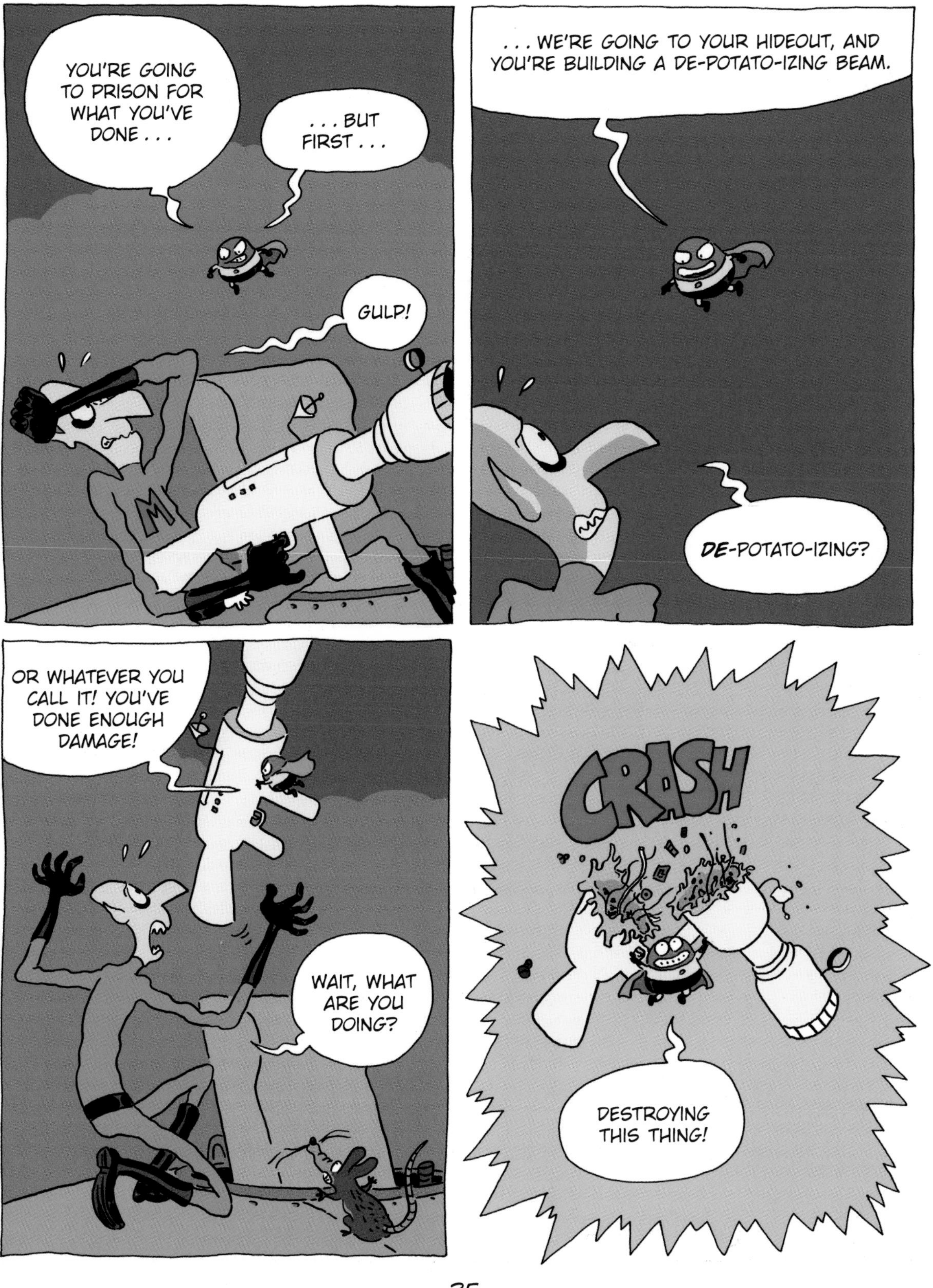
YOU'RE GOING TO PRISON FOR WHAT YOU'VE DONE . . .
. . . BUT FIRST . . .
GULP!
. . . WE'RE GOING TO YOUR HIDEOUT, AND YOU'RE BUILDING A DE-POTATO-IZING BEAM.
DE-POTATO-IZING?
OR WHATEVER YOU CALL IT! YOU'VE DONE ENOUGH DAMAGE!
WAIT, WHAT ARE YOU DOING?
CRASH
DESTROYING THIS THING!

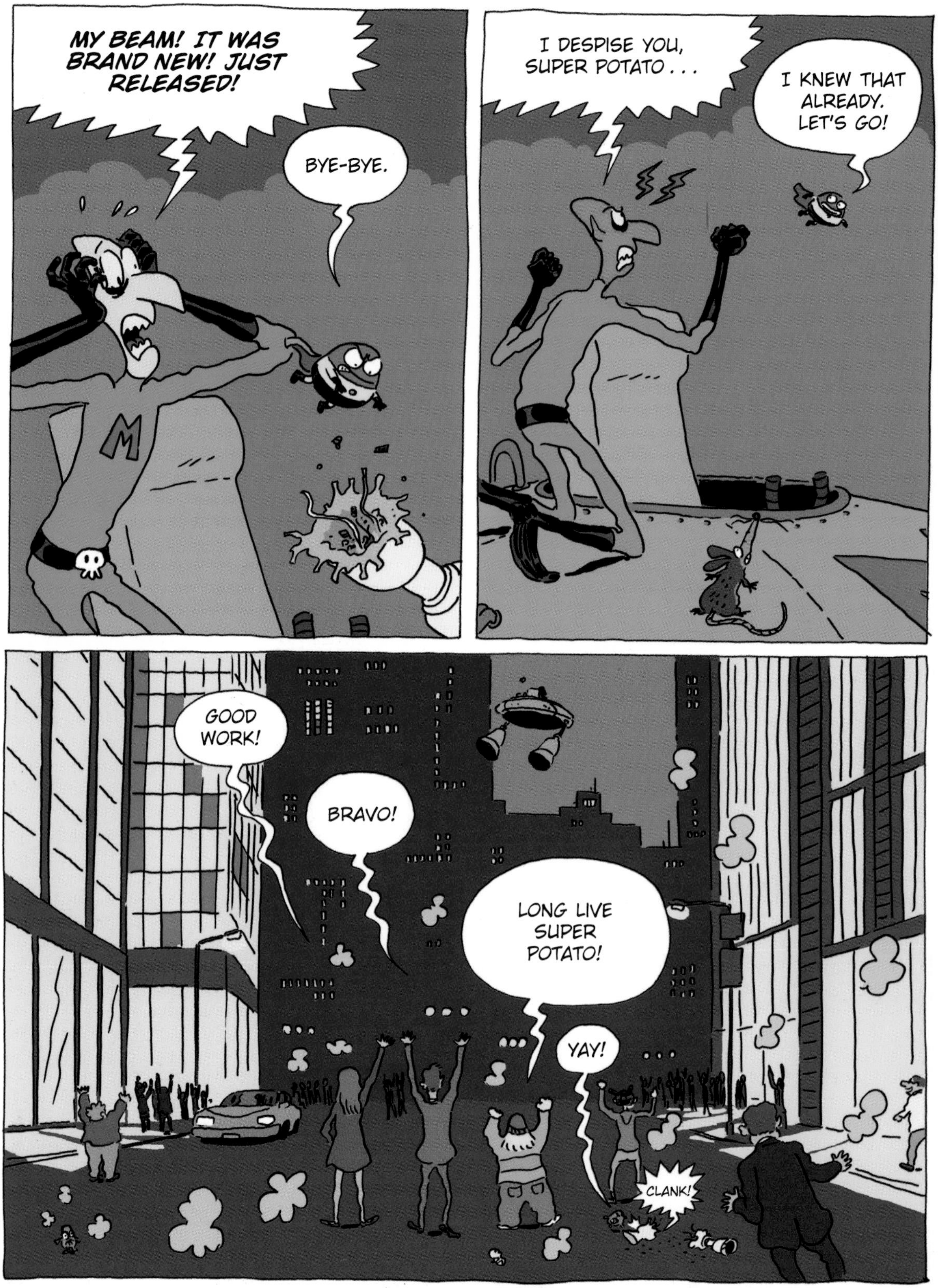

MY BEAM! IT WAS BRAND NEW! JUST RELEASED!
BYE-BYE.
I DESPISE YOU, SUPER POTATO . . .
I KNEW THAT ALREADY. LET'S GO!
GOOD WORK!
BRAVO!
LONG LIVE SUPER POTATO!
YAY!
CLANK!

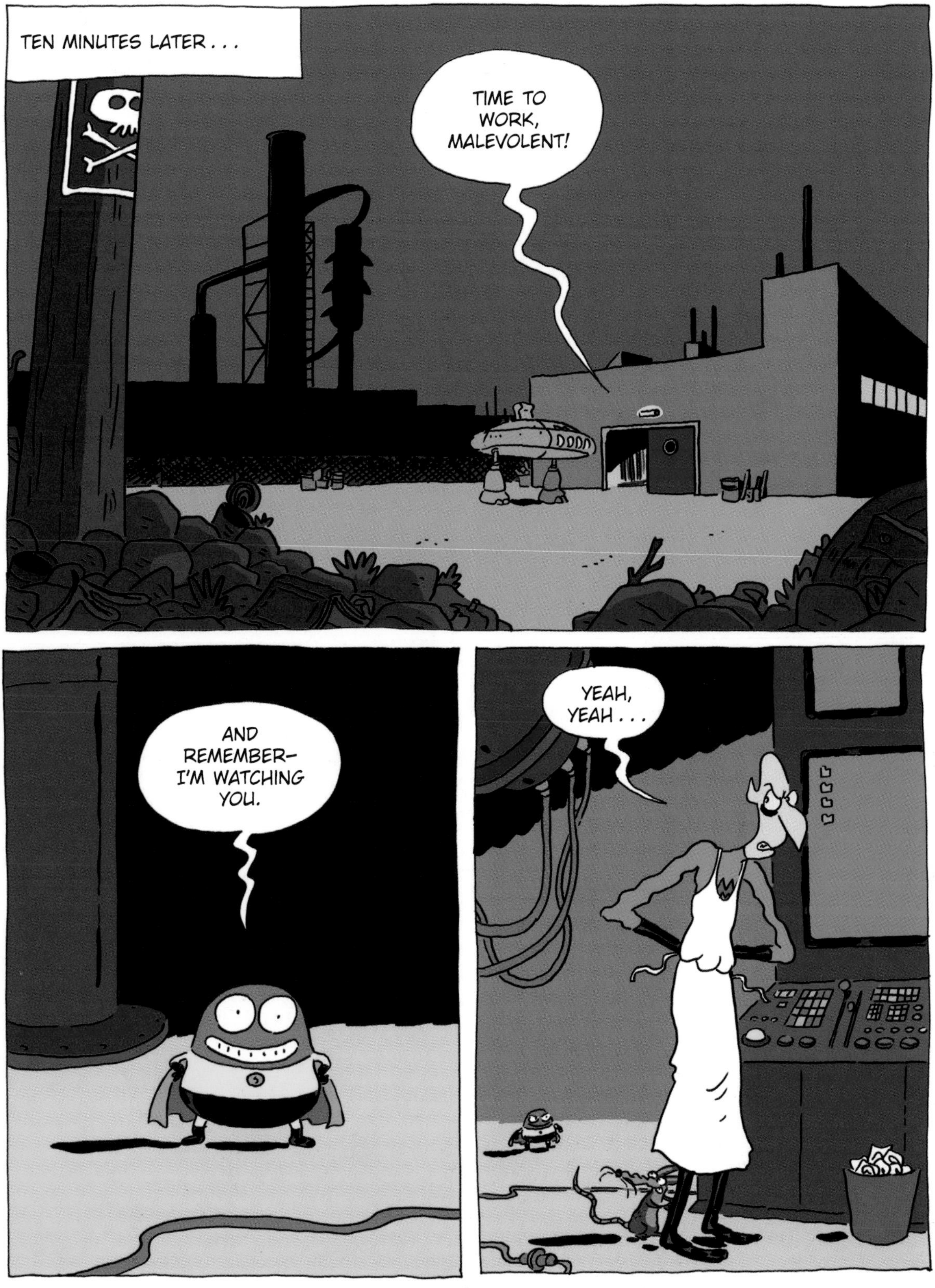
TEN MINUTES LATER . . .
TIME TO WORK, MALEVOLENT!
AND REMEMBER– I'M WATCHING YOU.
YEAH, YEAH . . .

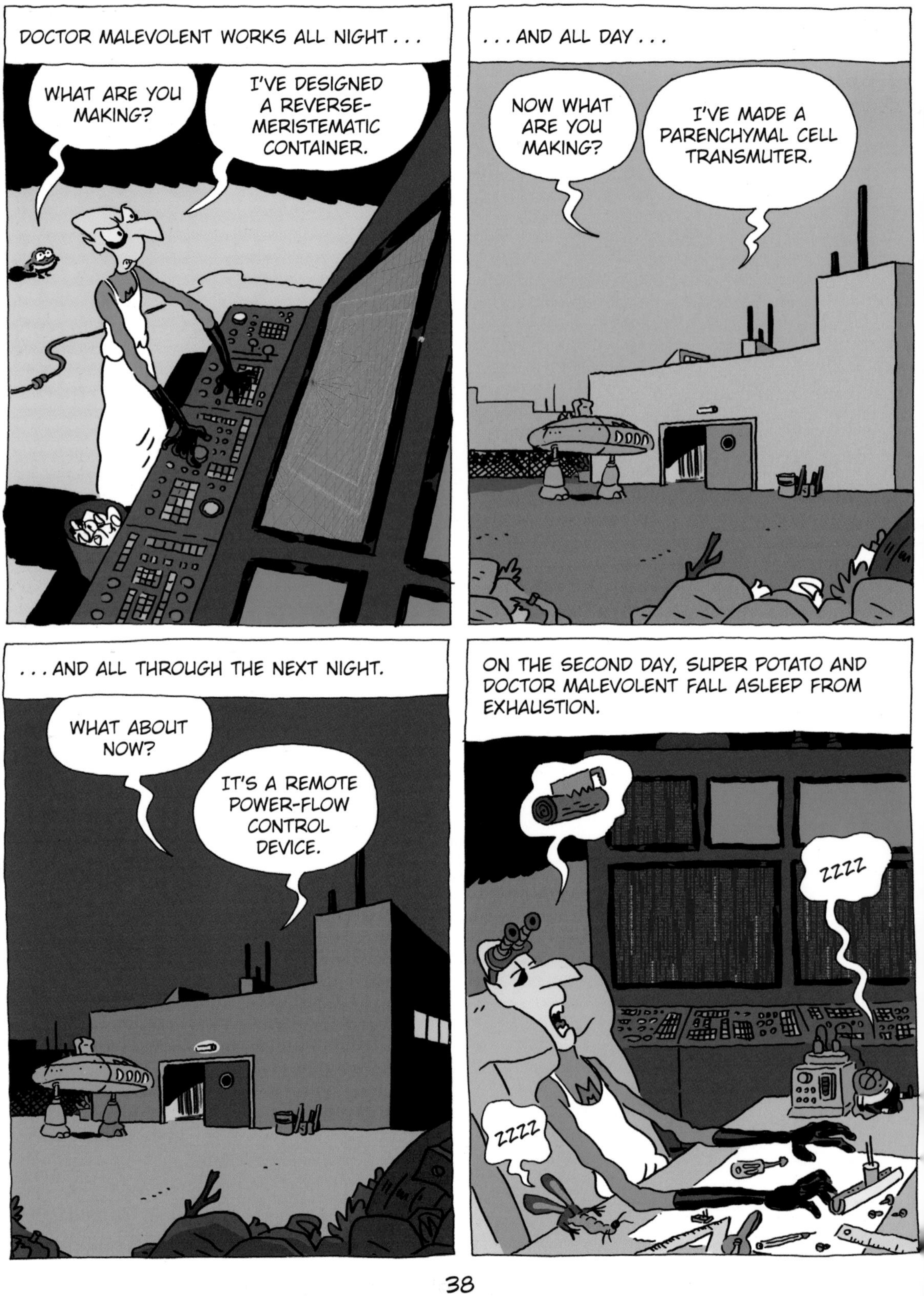
DOCTOR MALEVOLENT WORKS ALL NIGHT . . .
WHAT ARE YOU MAKING?
I'VE DESIGNED A REVERSE-MERISTEMATIC CONTAINER.
. . . AND ALL DAY . . .
NOW WHAT ARE YOU MAKING?
I'VE MADE A PARENCHYMAL CELL TRANSMUTER.
. . . AND ALL THROUGH THE NEXT NIGHT.
WHAT ABOUT NOW?
IT'S A REMOTE POWER-FLOW CONTROL DEVICE.
ON THE SECOND DAY, SUPER POTATO AND DOCTOR MALEVOLENT FALL ASLEEP FROM EXHAUSTION.
ZZZZ
ZZZZ

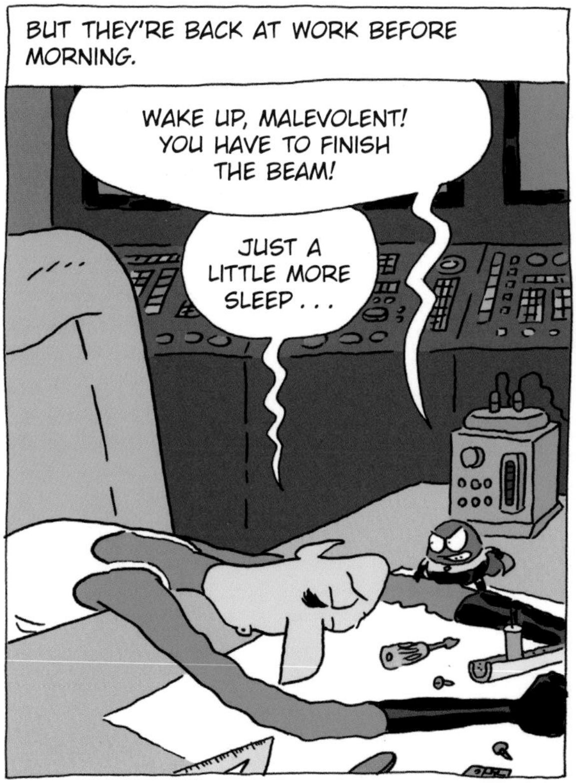
BUT THEY'RE BACK AT WORK BEFORE MORNING.
WAKE UP, MALEVOLENT! YOU HAVE TO FINISH THE BEAM!
JUST A LITTLE MORE SLEEP . . .

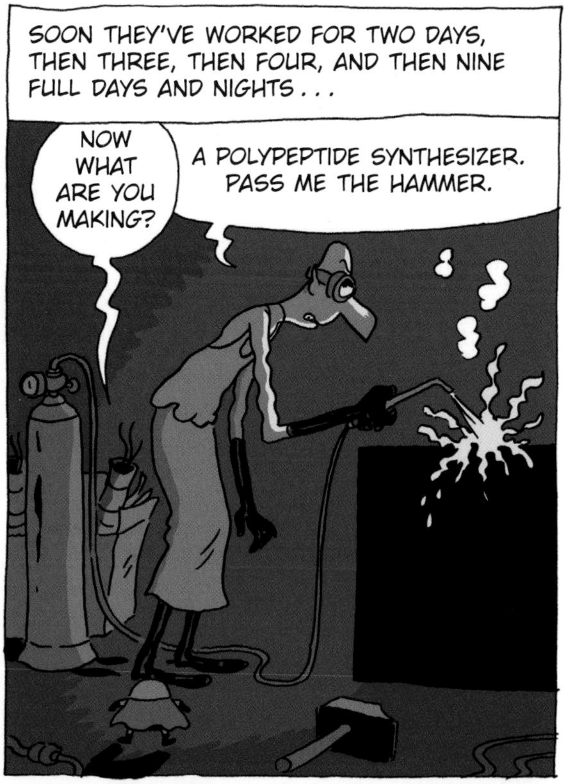
SOON THEY'VE WORKED FOR TWO DAYS, THEN THREE, THEN FOUR, AND THEN NINE FULL DAYS AND NIGHTS . . .
NOW WHAT ARE YOU MAKING?
A POLYPEPTIDE SYNTHESIZER. PASS ME THE HAMMER.

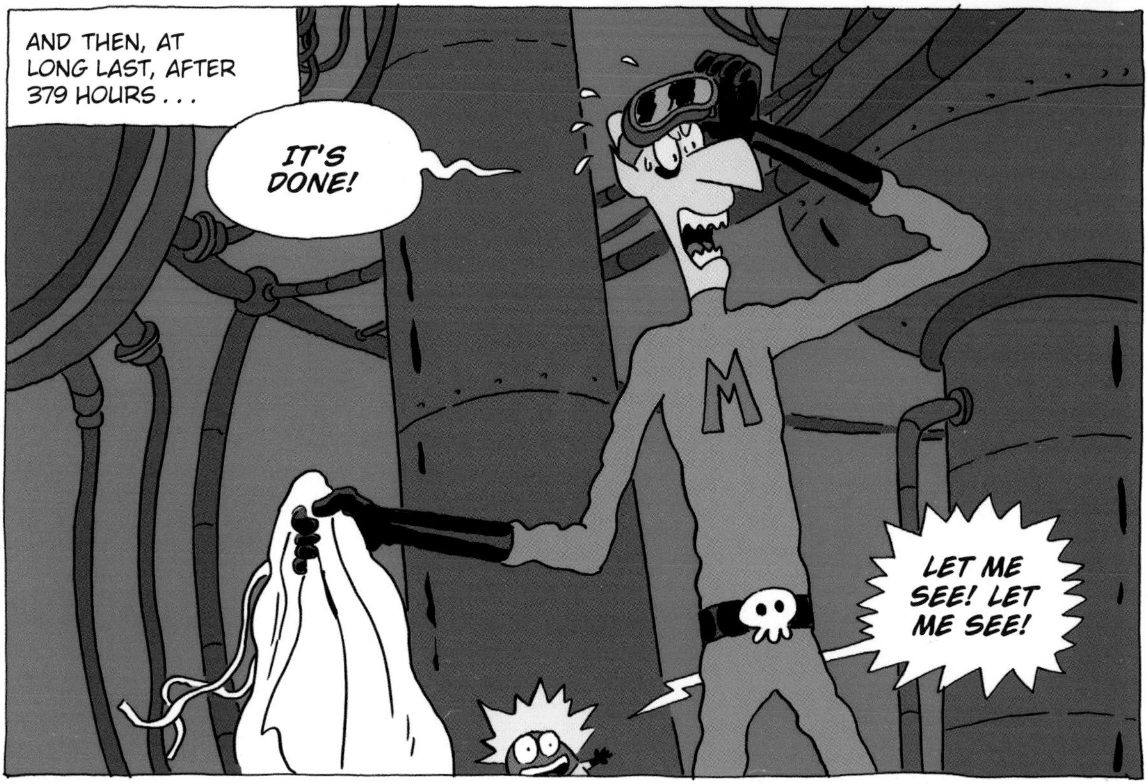
AND THEN, AT LONG LAST, AFTER 379 HOURS . . .
IT'S DONE!
LET ME SEE! LET ME SEE!

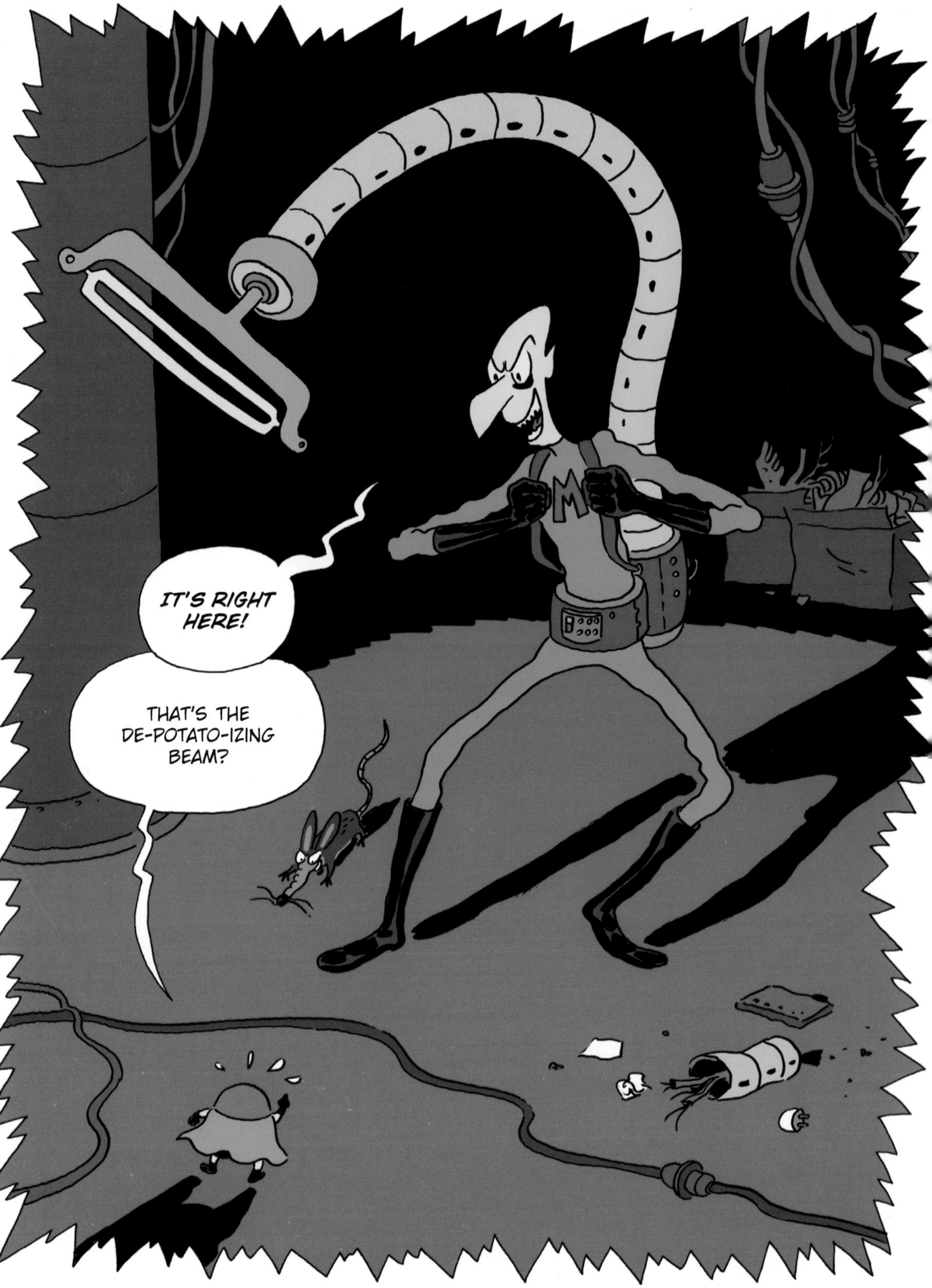

IT'S RIGHT HERE!
THAT'S THE DE-POTATO-IZING BEAM?

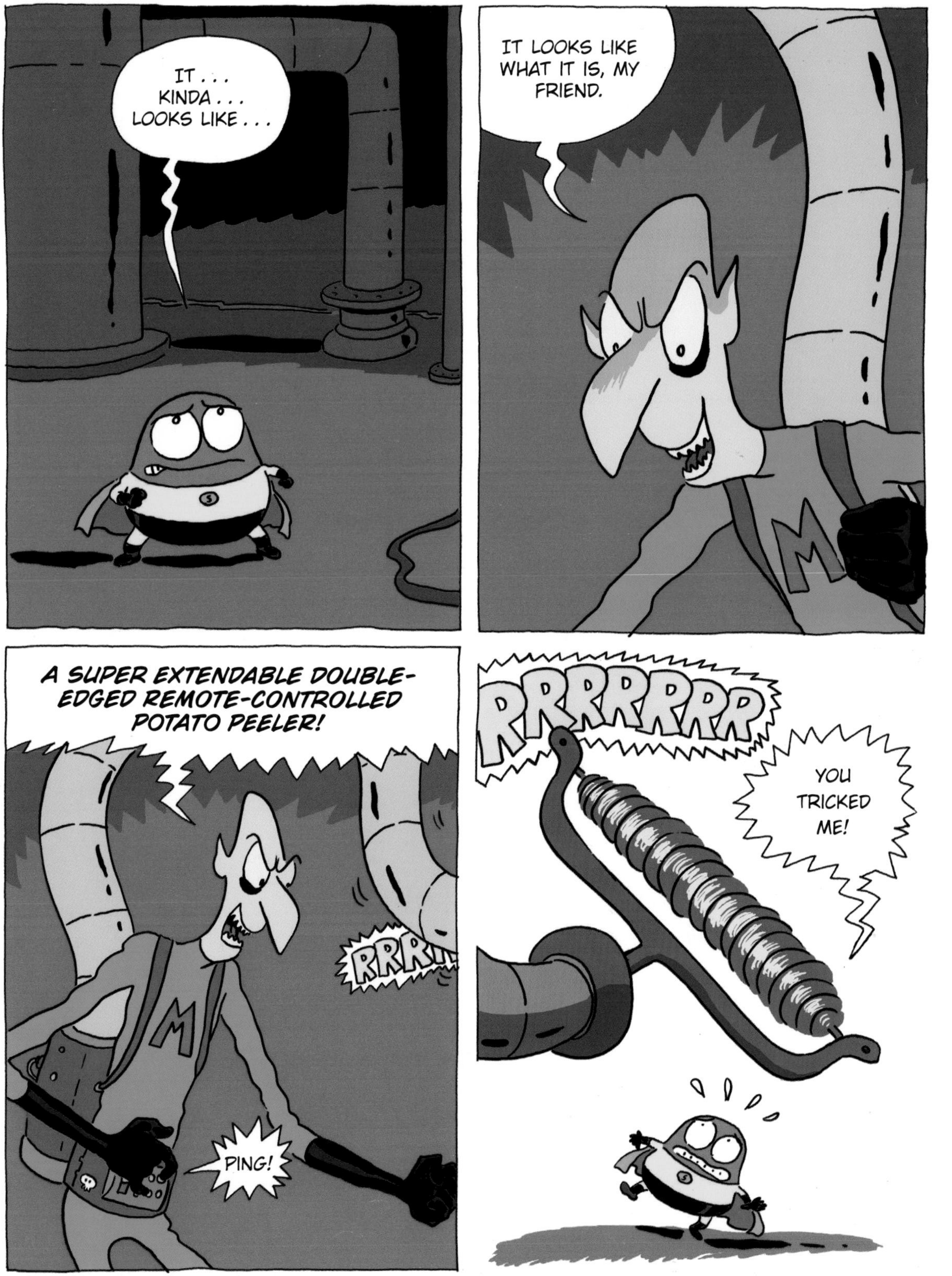
IT . . . KINDA . . . LOOKS LIKE . . .
IT LOOKS LIKE WHAT IT IS, MY FRIEND.
A SUPER EXTENDABLE DOUBLE-EDGED REMOTE-CONTROLLED POTATO PEELER!
RRR
PING!
RRRRRRRR
YOU TRICKED ME!

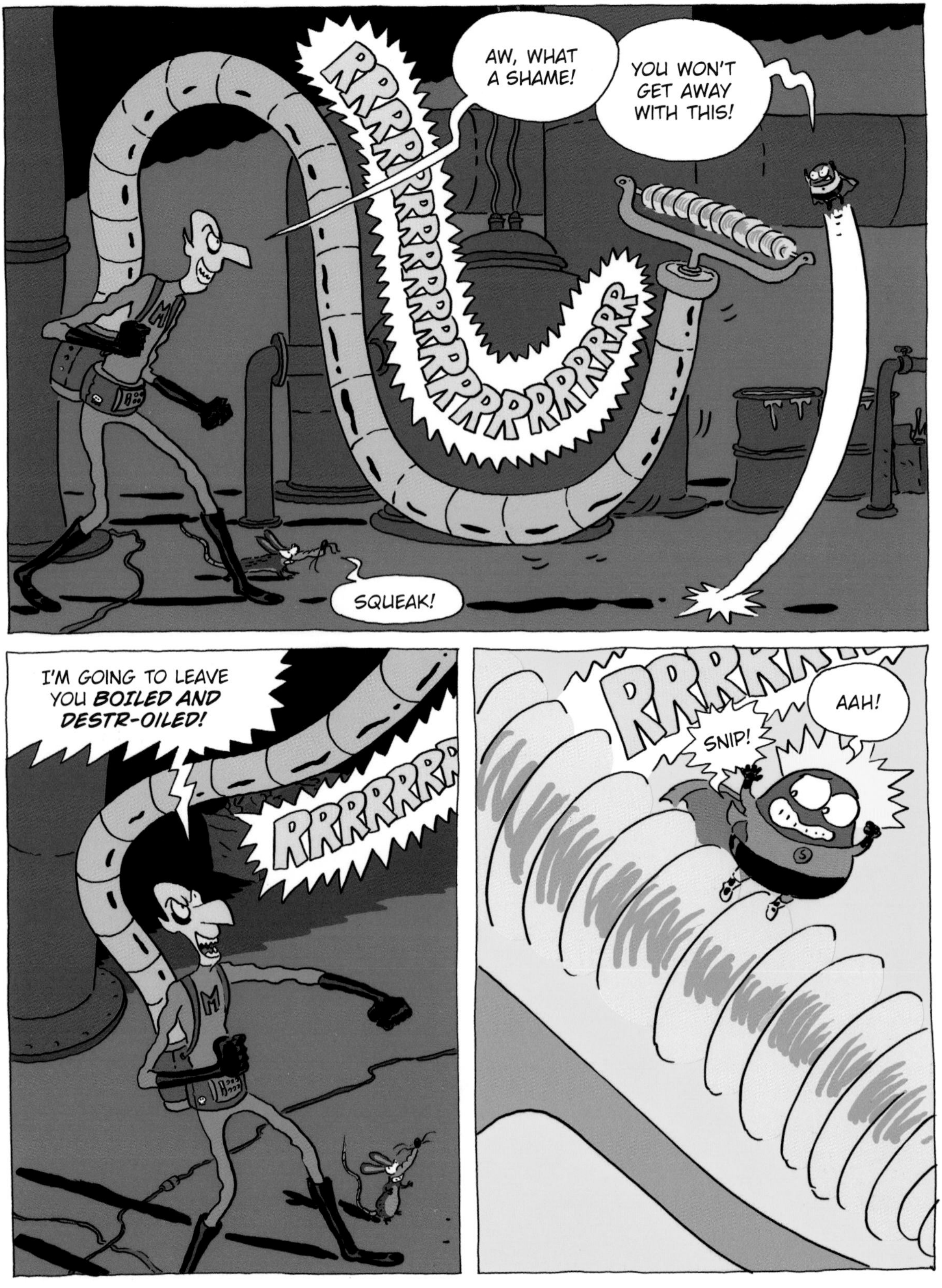
RRRRRRRRRRRRRRRRRRRRRRRRRRRRRR
AW, WHAT A SHAME!
YOU WON'T GET AWAY WITH THIS!
SQUEAK!
I'M GOING TO LEAVE YOU **BOILED AND DESTR-OILED!**
RRRRRRR
SNIP!
AAH!

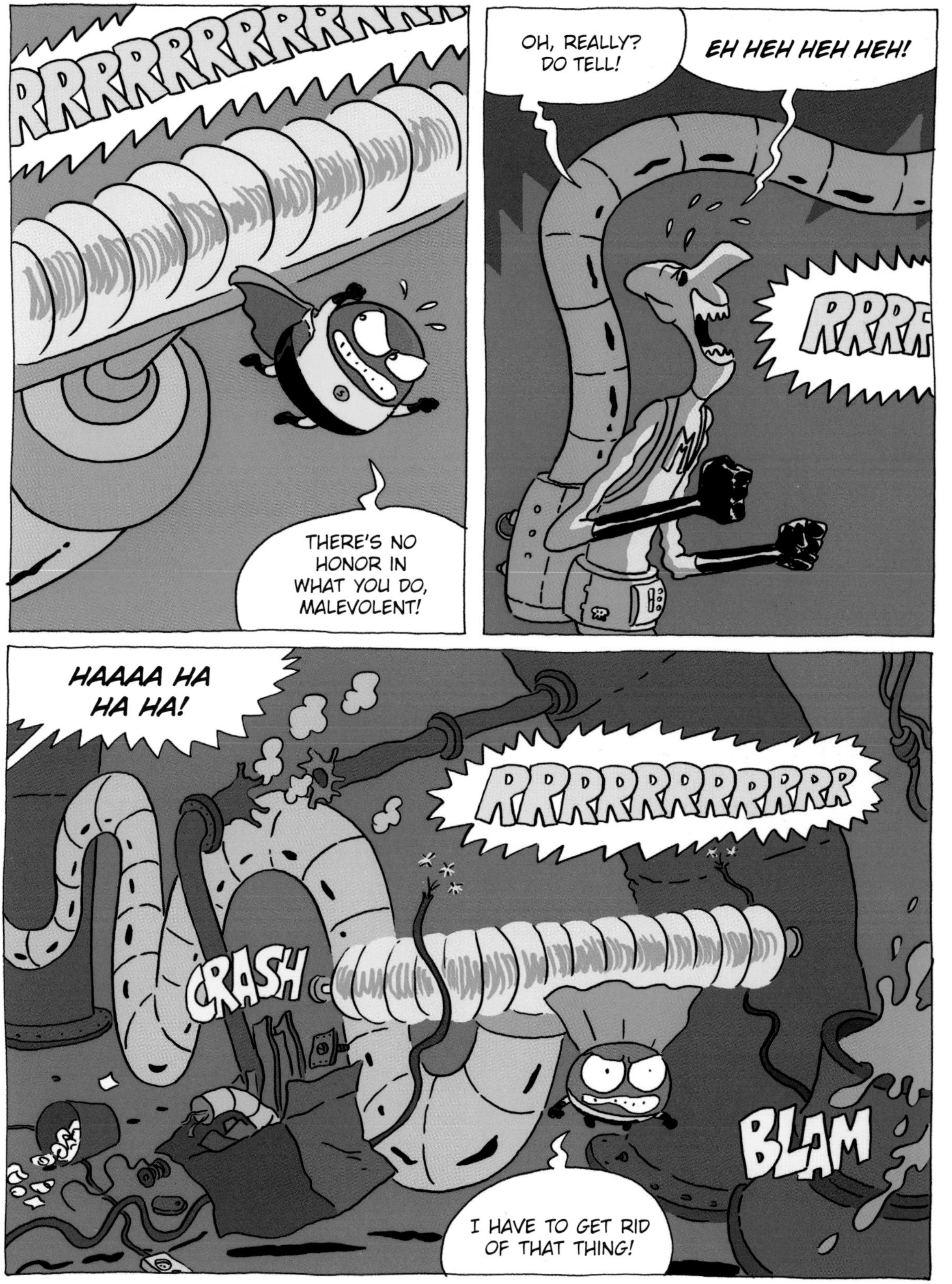
RRRRRRRRRRRRRRRR
THERE'S NO HONOR IN WHAT YOU DO, MALEVOLENT!
OH, REALLY? DO TELL!
EH HEH HEH HEH!
RRRR
HAAAA HA HA HA!
RRRRRRRRRRRRR
CRASH
BLAM
I HAVE TO GET RID OF THAT THING!

DOCTOR MALEVOLENT, IN HIS QUEST TO FINISH OFF SUPER POTATO...

AHA HA HA HA!

...DOESN'T SEE THAT HE'S TRASHING HIS OWN LABORATORY.

RRRRR

THAT'S IT, KEEP FOLLOWING ME.

AND THE DOCTOR SHOULD BE CAREFUL AROUND HIS LABORATORY, BECAUSE IF NOT...

BLAM

SODIUM.

CRASH

WATER.

BLA

HOLD ON, HERE'S A SCIENTIST TO EXPLAIN WHAT HAPPENS WHEN SODIUM MIXES WITH WATER.

AS A CHEMICAL ELEMENT, SODIUM IS HIGHLY UNSTABLE, MUCH LIKE CERTAIN PEOPLE IN THIS STORY. ITS REACTION MECHANISM WITH WATER IS $2Na_{(S)} + 2H_2O \rightarrow 2NaOH_{(AQ)} + H_{2(G)}$.

WELL, ANYWAY, THAT MEANS YOU CAN PRODUCE...

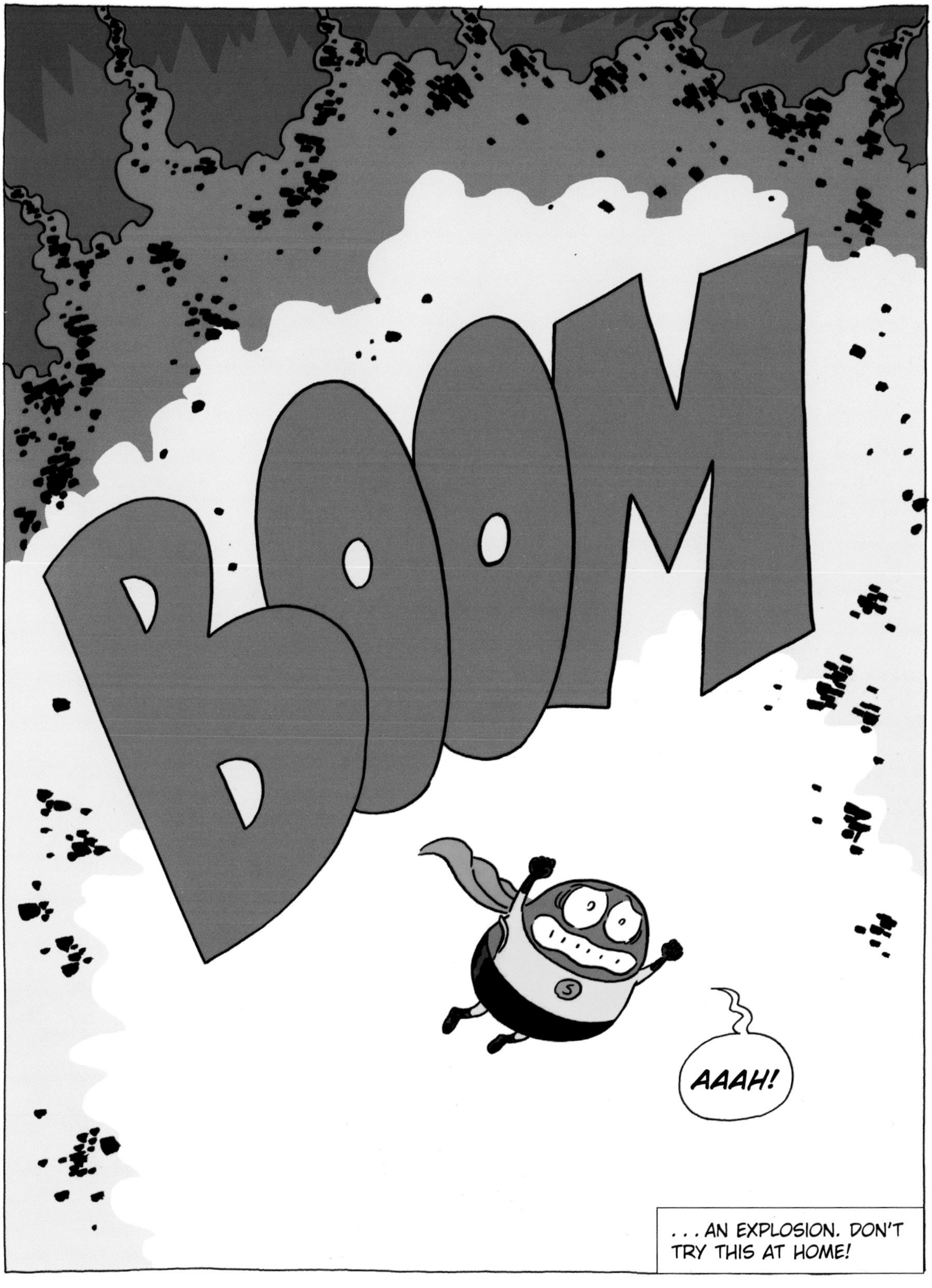
BOOM
AAAH!
. . . AN EXPLOSION. DON'T TRY THIS AT HOME!

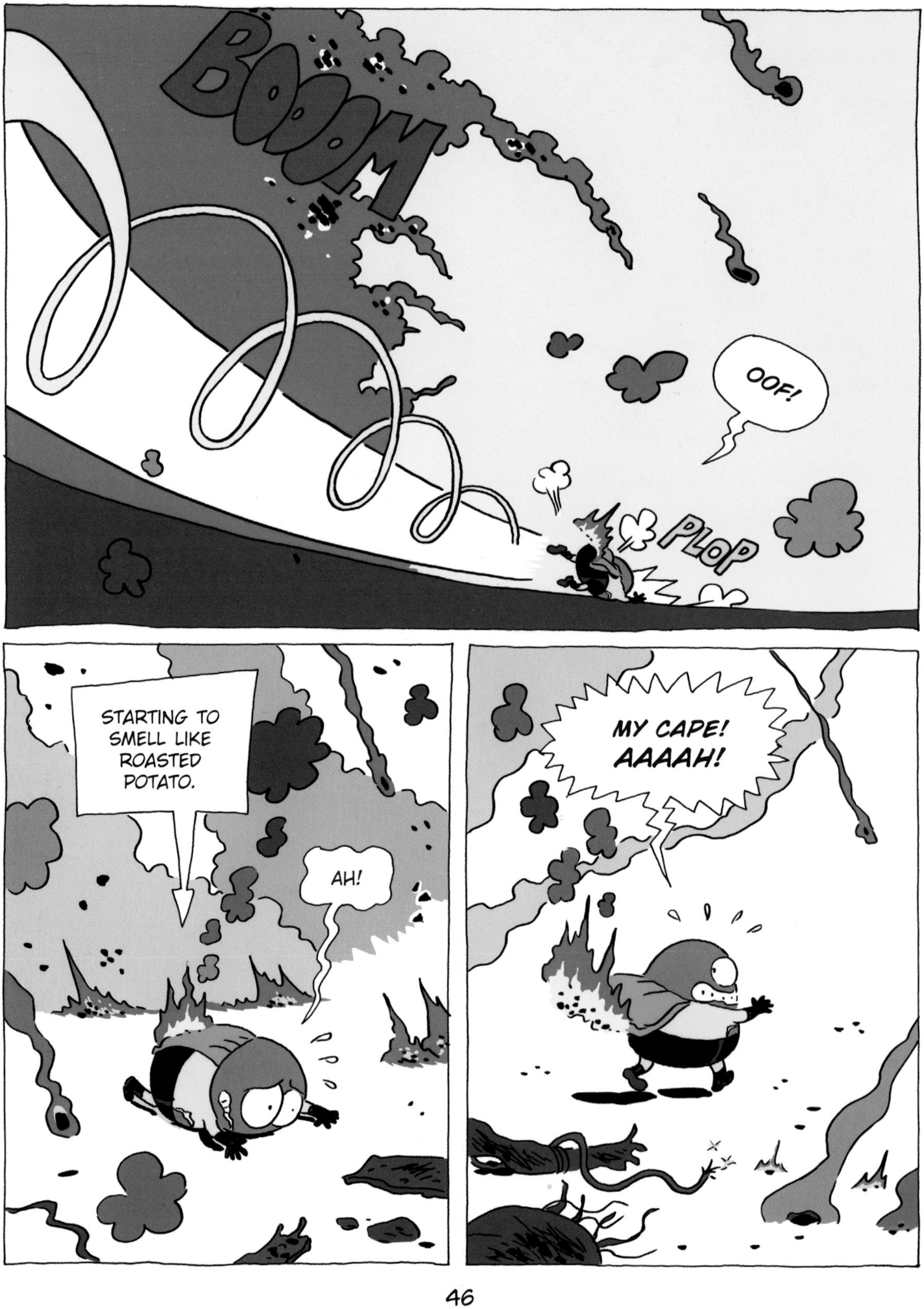
BOOOM
OOF!
PLOP
STARTING TO SMELL LIKE ROASTED POTATO.
AH!
MY CAPE! AAAAH!

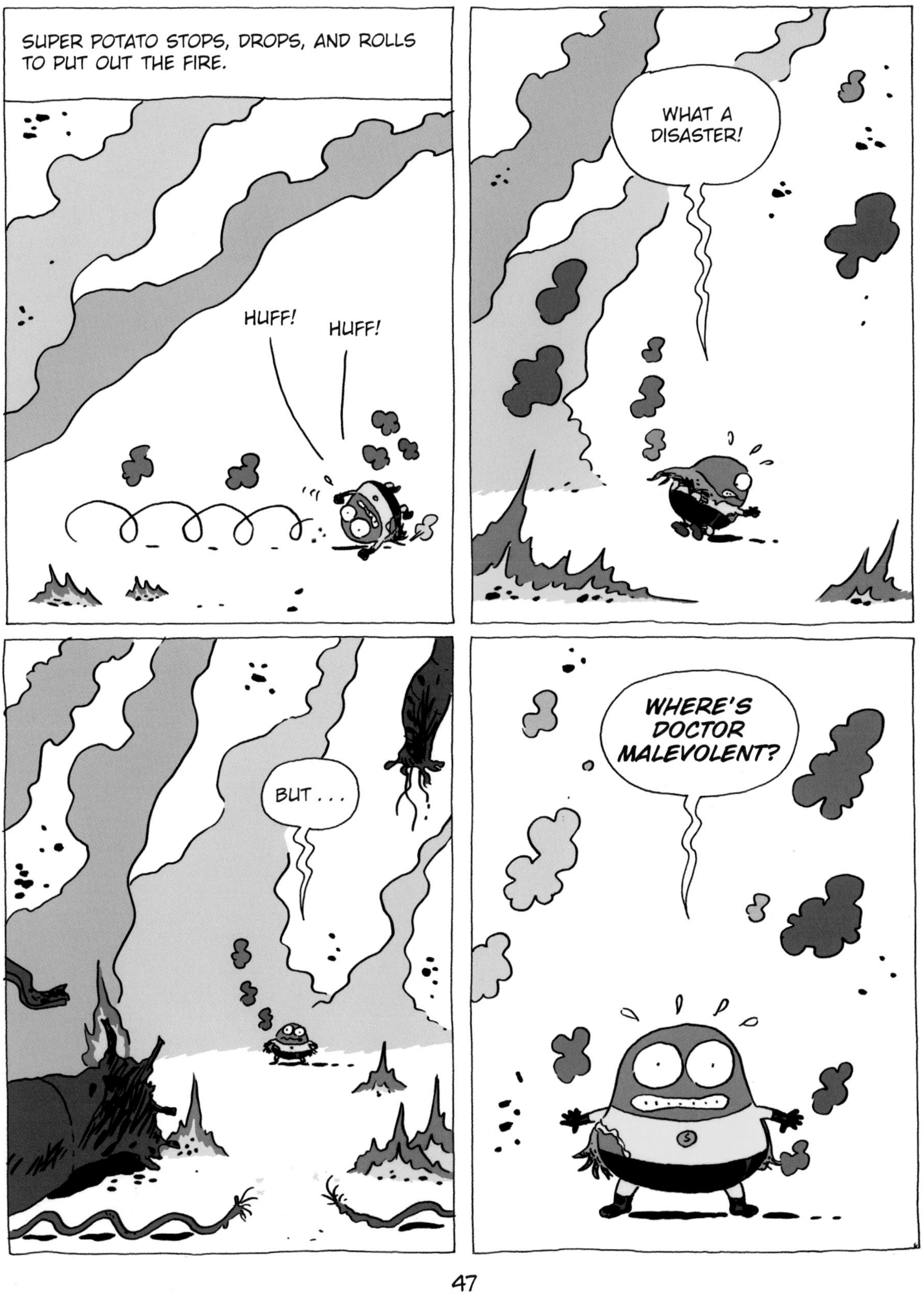
SUPER POTATO STOPS, DROPS, AND ROLLS TO PUT OUT THE FIRE.
HUFF!
HUFF!
WHAT A DISASTER!
BUT . . .
WHERE'S DOCTOR MALEVOLENT?

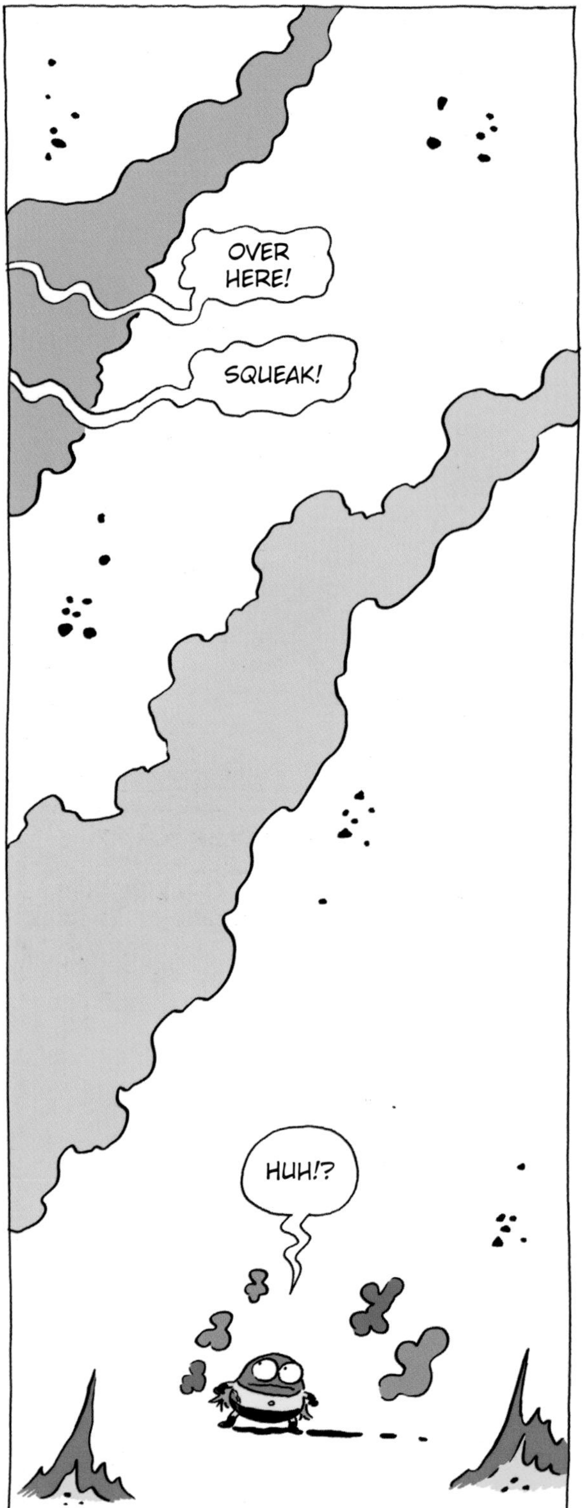
OVER HERE!
SQUEAK!
HUH!?

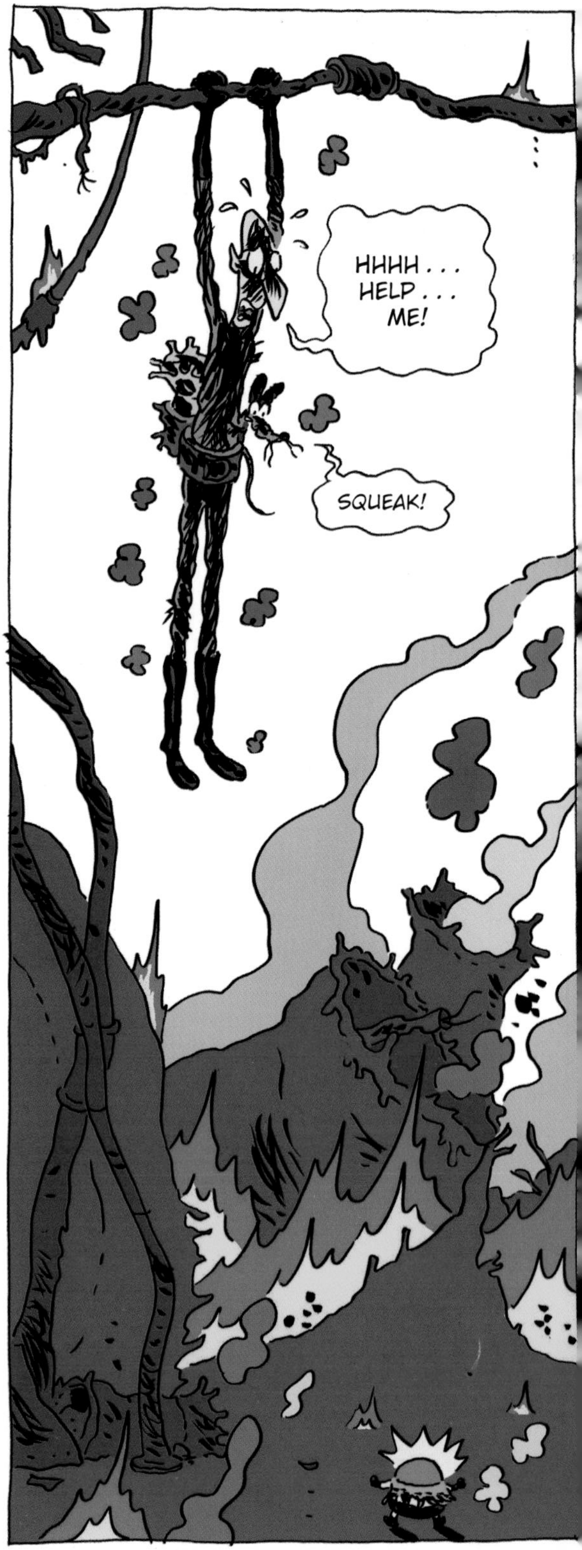
HHHH . . . HELP . . . ME!
SQUEAK!

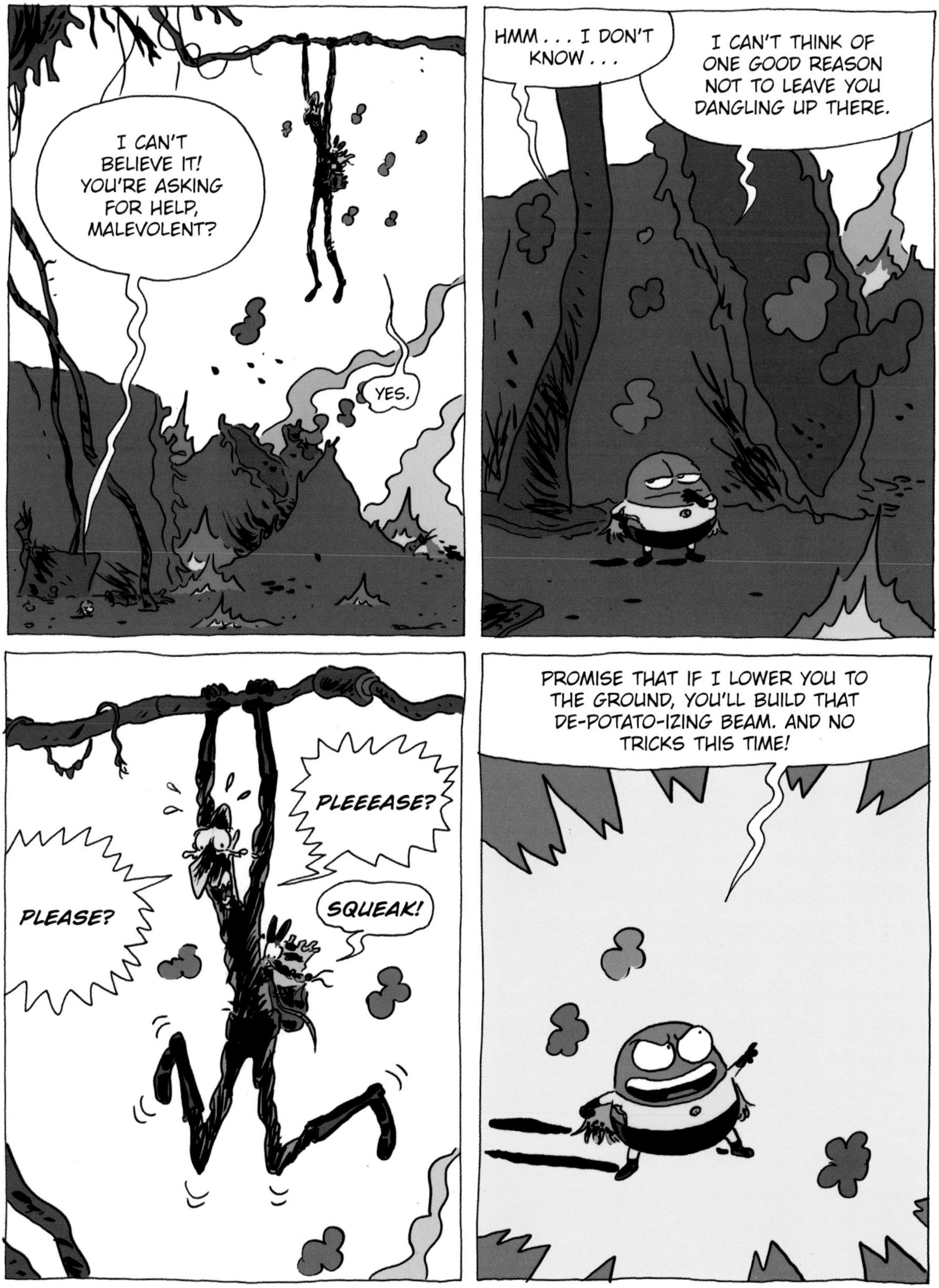
I CAN'T BELIEVE IT! YOU'RE ASKING FOR HELP, MALEVOLENT?
YES.
HMM . . . I DON'T KNOW . . .
I CAN'T THINK OF ONE GOOD REASON NOT TO LEAVE YOU DANGLING UP THERE.
PLEASE?
PLEEEASE?
SQUEAK!
PROMISE THAT IF I LOWER YOU TO THE GROUND, YOU'LL BUILD THAT DE-POTATO-IZING BEAM. AND NO TRICKS THIS TIME!

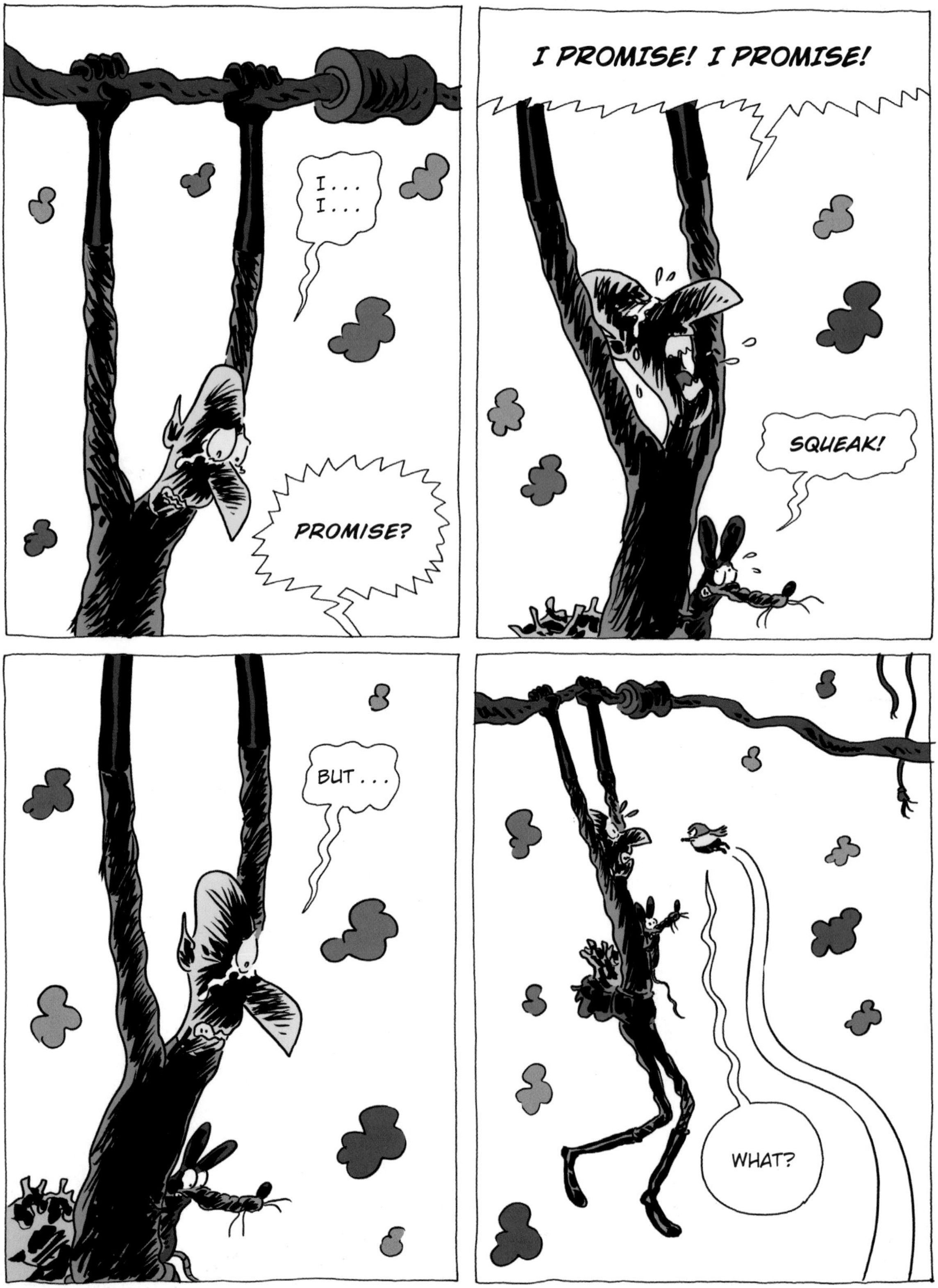
I . . .
I . . .
PROMISE?
I PROMISE! I PROMISE!
SQUEAK!
BUT . . .
WHAT?

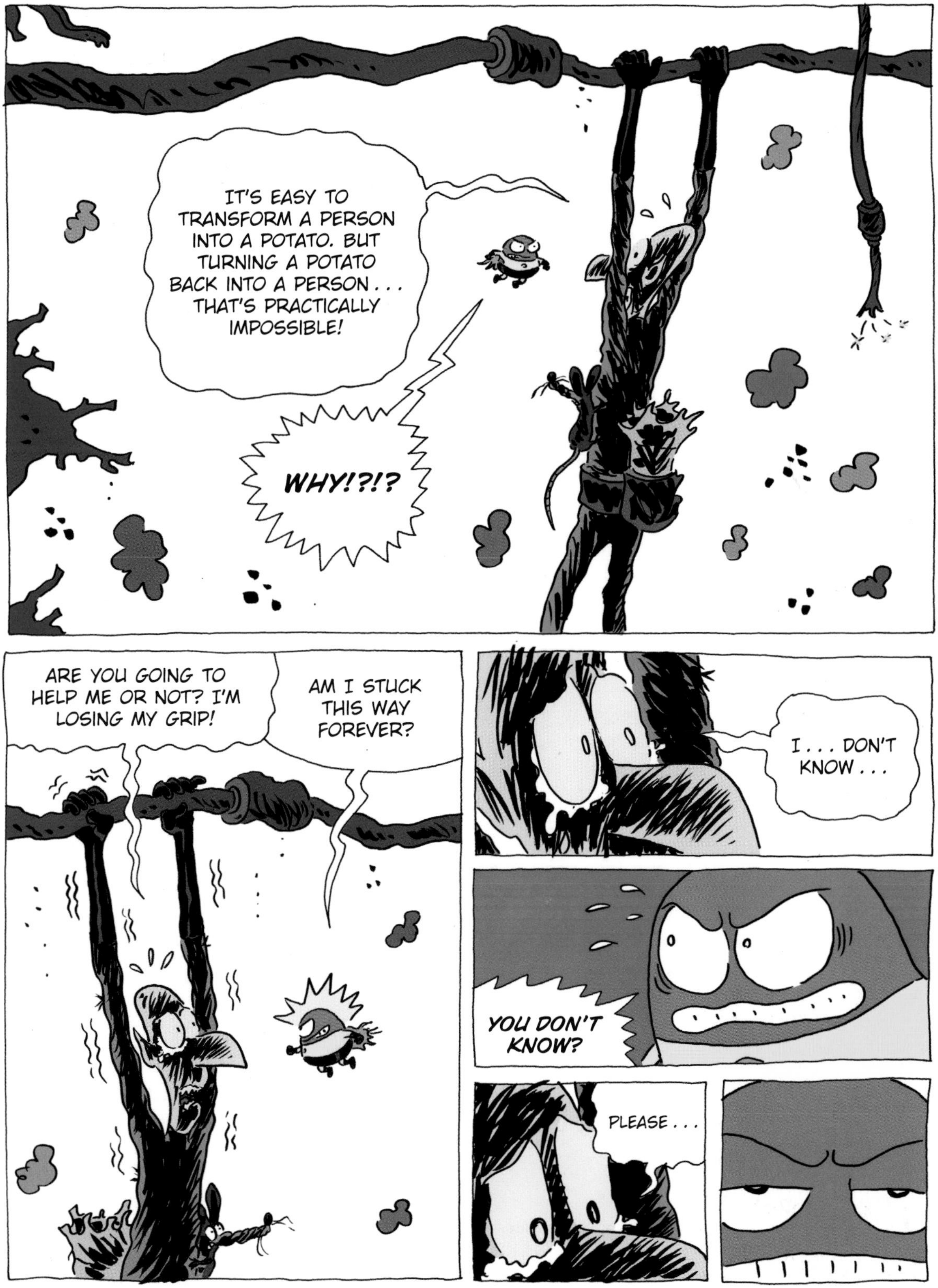
IT'S EASY TO TRANSFORM A PERSON INTO A POTATO. BUT TURNING A POTATO BACK INTO A PERSON . . . THAT'S PRACTICALLY IMPOSSIBLE!
WHY!?!?
ARE YOU GOING TO HELP ME OR NOT? I'M LOSING MY GRIP!
AM I STUCK THIS WAY FOREVER?
I . . . DON'T KNOW . . .
YOU DON'T KNOW?
PLEASE . . .

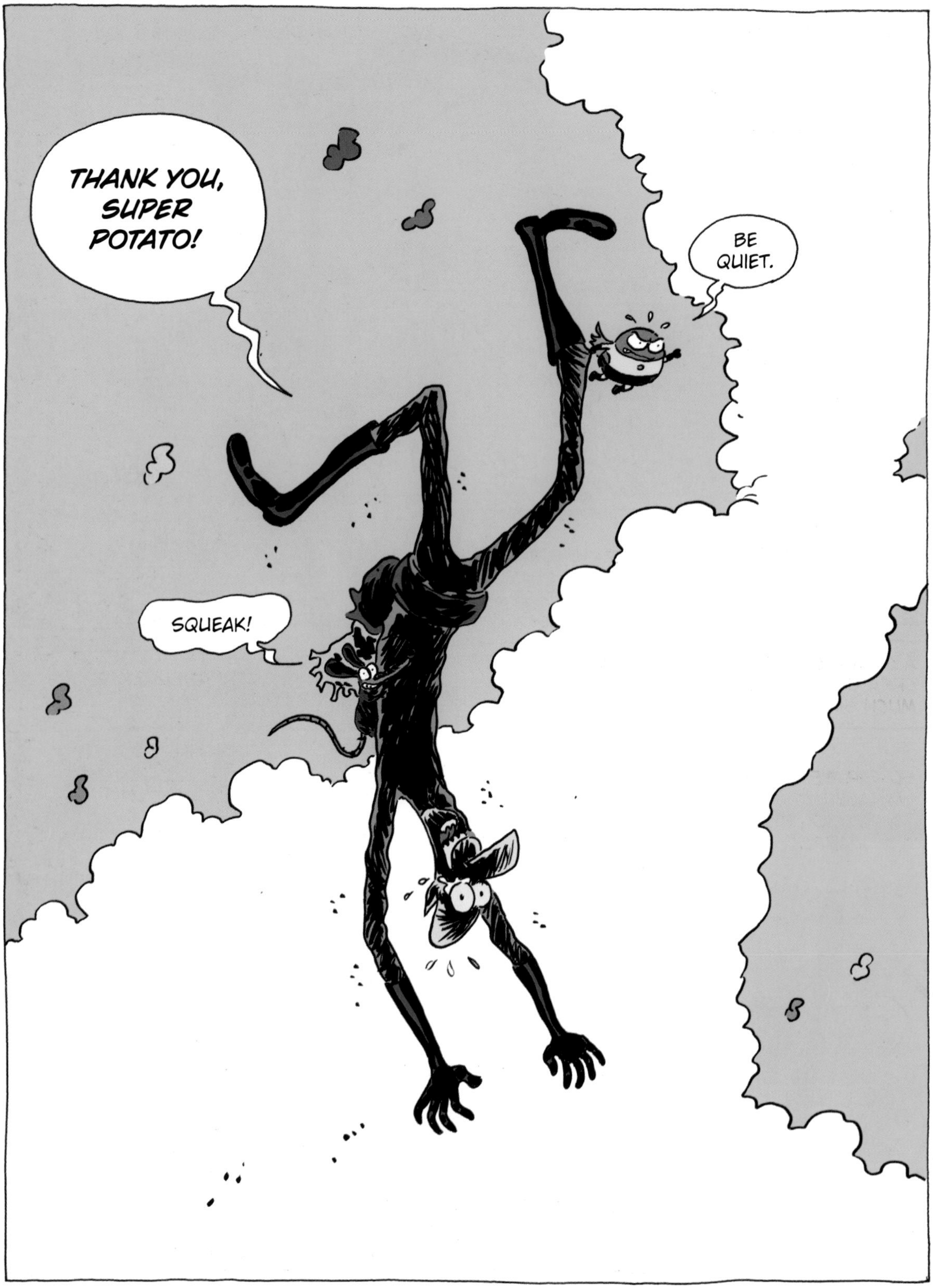
THANK YOU, SUPER POTATO!
BE QUIET.
SQUEAK!

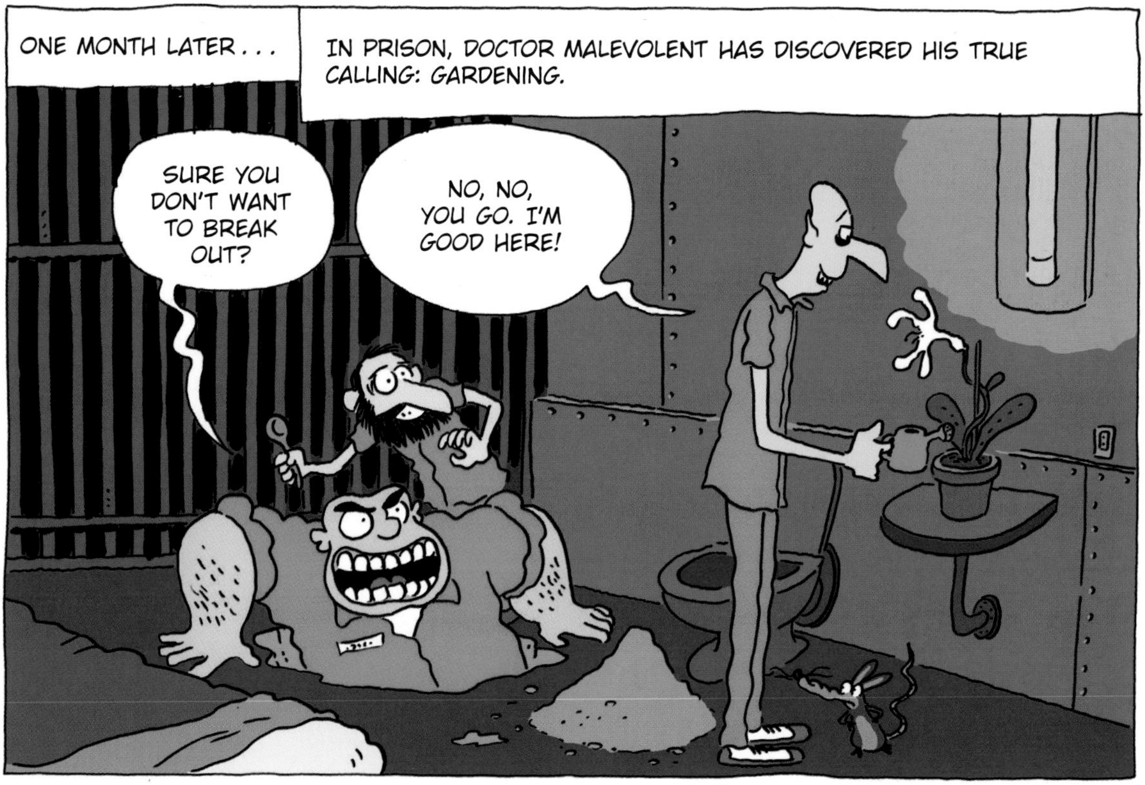
ONE MONTH LATER . . .
IN PRISON, DOCTOR MALEVOLENT HAS DISCOVERED HIS TRUE CALLING: GARDENING.
SURE YOU DON'T WANT TO BREAK OUT?
NO, NO, YOU GO. I'M GOOD HERE!

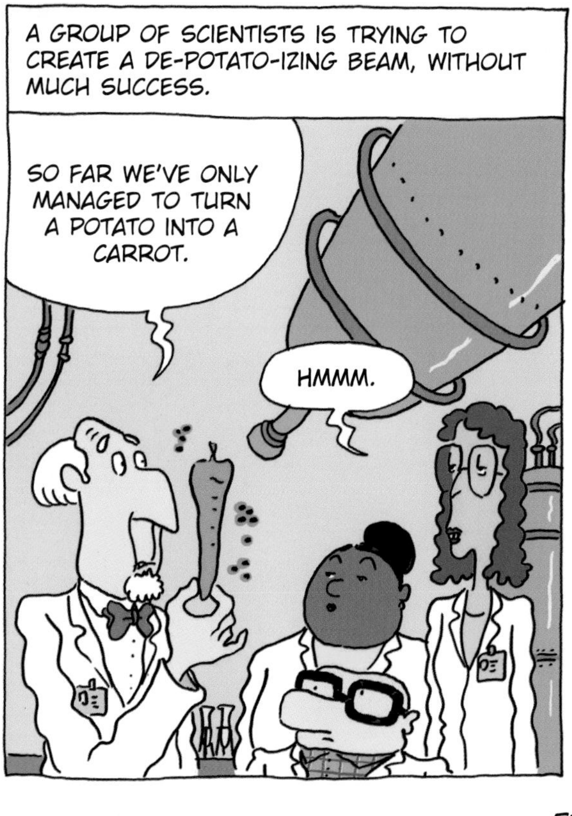
A GROUP OF SCIENTISTS IS TRYING TO CREATE A DE-POTATO-IZING BEAM, WITHOUT MUCH SUCCESS.
SO FAR WE'VE ONLY MANAGED TO TURN A POTATO INTO A CARROT.
HMMM.

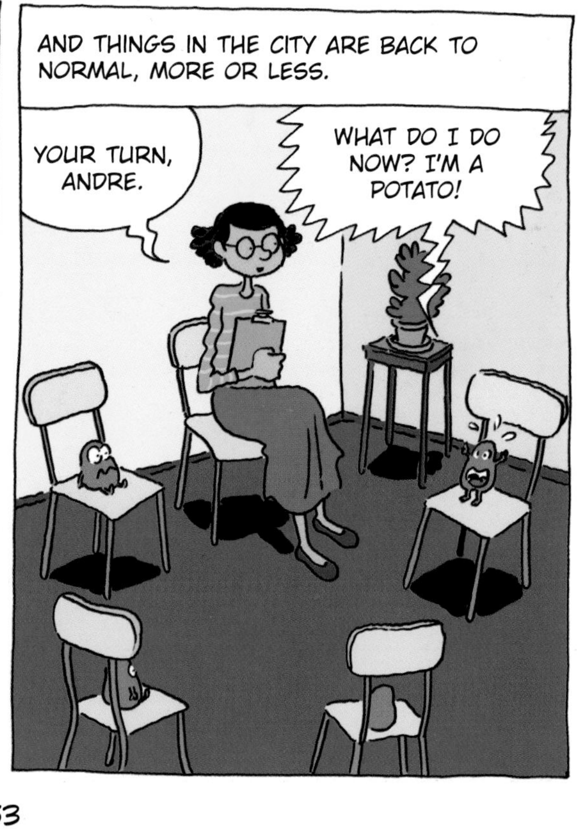
AND THINGS IN THE CITY ARE BACK TO NORMAL, MORE OR LESS.
YOUR TURN, ANDRE.
WHAT DO I DO NOW? I'M A POTATO!

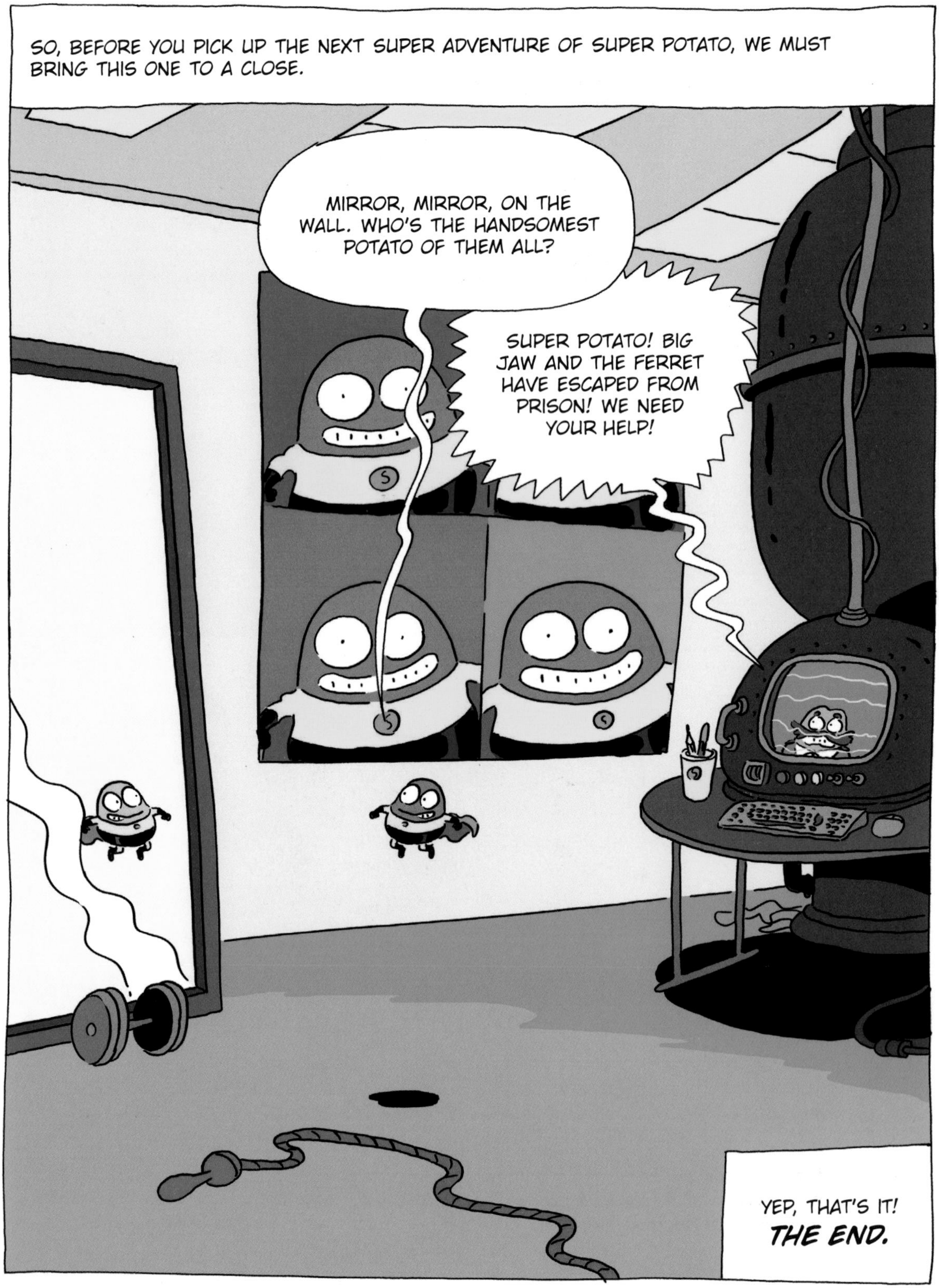
SO, BEFORE YOU PICK UP THE NEXT SUPER ADVENTURE OF SUPER POTATO, WE MUST BRING THIS ONE TO A CLOSE.
MIRROR, MIRROR, ON THE WALL. WHO'S THE HANDSOMEST POTATO OF THEM ALL?
SUPER POTATO! BIG JAW AND THE FERRET HAVE ESCAPED FROM PRISON! WE NEED YOUR HELP!
YEP, THAT'S IT!
THE END.

SUPER POTATO

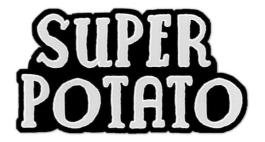

Available soon:
The second adventure in the Super Potato saga,

SUPER POTATO'S GALACTIC BREAKOUT

SUPER POTATO
#2
SUPER POTATO'S
GALACTIC BREAKOUT

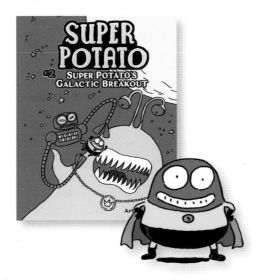

TRAPPED—IN AN OUTER SPACE ZOO!

Zort the Third is an alien king with a rude hobby. He zooms through space, capturing new breeds for his collection of rare creatures. He has a Buzzillion from Planet Buzz and a Zazzarina from Planet Zazz. But when he snags Earth's top superhero, he gets more than he bargained for.

Zort's about to learn what happens when you cage a crime fighter. Because no zoo—on Earth or in space—can hold Super Potato. Our hero is planning an escape that will turn the galaxy upside down. It's time for Super Potato to break out!

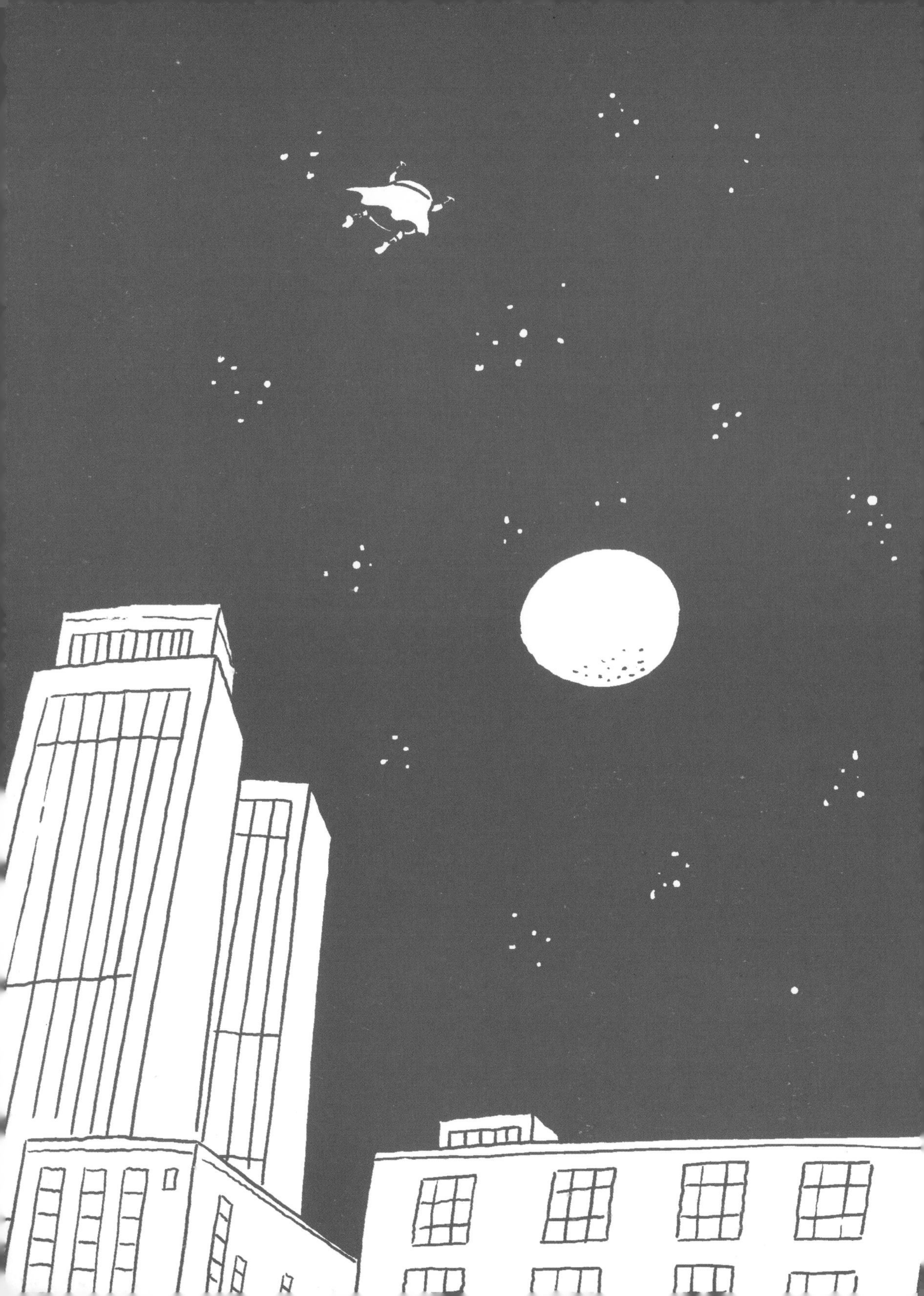